"Why should ~~you~~ ~~way~~
like this ~~for someone you haven~~
know?"

Whitney had to understand his motives. First saving her from drowning and rescuing her car, and now helping her find a place to stay.

"I did have a hand in saving your life, so that gives us a kind of bond," he told her. "I also want you to be happy living the life I saved."

The man was practically a saint. Excited, relieved and feeling almost euphoric, Whitney threw her arms around his neck and declared, "You're a lifesaver." She said it a second before she kissed him.

She only meant for it to be a quick pass of her lips against his, the kind of kiss one good friend gives another. But at the last second, Liam turned his head just a fraction closer in her direction. What began as a fleeting kiss turned into a great deal more.

Something of substance and depth.

The exuberance she had initially felt stole her breath. Her body suddenly ignited, and had his arms not gone around her when they did, she would *not* be standing up right now. A wave of weakness snaked through her, robbing her of the ability to stand. Forcing her to cling to him in order to remain upright.

She *shouldn't* be doing this.

Dear Reader,

Welcome back to Forever, that tiny Texas town filled with men and women whose hearts are as big as the state they live in. It's a town where everyone not only knows your name, but pretty much everything else about you.

In the two previous Forever books, we've met and watched two of the Murphy men find the women of their dreams. This time, the last of the Murphy men *saves* the woman of his dreams when Whitney Marlowe is caught up in a flash flood that engulfs her car—and her. Unable to swim, she screams for help, but is certain that she's done for. Lucky for her, she's wrong. And lucky for the musically inclined Liam Murphy, the woman he'd just saved from a watery grave just happens to be in the music business. But can Liam help her overcome her fear of involvement and win her over to his side? Come and watch a confirmed bachelor happily lose his heart while he tries to gain a career.

As always, I thank you for reading, and from the bottom of my heart, I wish you someone to love who loves you back.

All the best,

Marie Ferrarella

CHRISTMAS COWBOY DUET

—

Marie Ferrarella

HARLEQUIN® AMERICAN ROMANCE®

Recycling programs
for this product may
not exist in your area.

ISBN-13: 978-0-373-75548-6

Christmas Cowboy Duet

Printed in U.S.A.

ABOUT THE AUTHOR

This *USA TODAY* bestselling and RITA® Award-winning author has written more than two hundred books for Harlequin, some under the name Marie Nicole. Her romances are beloved by fans worldwide. Visit her website, www.marieferrarella.com.

Books by Marie Ferrarella

HARLEQUIN AMERICAN ROMANCE

FOREVER, TEXAS
THE SHERIFF'S CHRISTMAS SURPRISE
RAMONA AND THE RENEGADE
THE DOCTOR'S FOREVER FAMILY
LASSOING THE DEPUTY
A BABY ON THE RANCH
A FOREVER CHRISTMAS
HIS FOREVER VALENTINE
A SMALL TOWN THANKSGIVING
THE COWBOY'S CHRISTMAS SURPRISE
HER FOREVER COWBOY
COWBOY FOR HIRE

HARLEQUIN SPECIAL EDITION

MATCHMAKING MAMAS
WISH UPON A MATCHMAKER
DATING FOR TWO
DIAMOND IN THE RUFF

Other titles by this author available in ebook format.

To
Dr. Seric Cusick,
the E.R. physician
who sewed my face back together.
Thank you!

Prologue

She'd never learned how to swim.

Somehow, there never seemed to be the right time to sneak in lessons.

Since she was born and bred in Los Angeles, close to an ocean and many pools, everyone just assumed she knew how to swim. It was a given. There were all those beaches, all that tempting water seductively lapping against the shore during those glorious endless summers.

But Whitney Marlowe had never had the time nor the inclination to get swimming lessons. Something more pressing always snagged her attention.

For as long as Whitney could remember, she'd always had this little voice inside of her head urging her on, whispering about goals that had yet to be met.

Swimming was recreational. Swimming was associated with fun. Even growing up, Whitney never seemed to have time for fun, except maybe for a few minutes at a time. A child of divorce, she was far too involved in making a name for herself to dwell on recreation. Everyone in her family was driven and it seemed as if from the very first moment of her life, she had been embroiled in one competition or another.

Oh, she dearly loved her siblings, all five of them, but she loved them just a tiny bit more whenever she could best them at something. It didn't matter what, as long as she could come out the winner.

Her father had promoted this spirit of competition, telling his children that it would better equip them when they went out into the world. He'd been a hard taskmaster.

But right now, all those goals, all those triumphant moments, none of them mattered. None of them meant anything because the sum total of all that wasn't going to save her.

This was it, Whitney thought in frantic despair.

This was the place where she was going to die. Outside of a town that hadn't even been much more than an imperceptible dot on her map. A stupid little town prophetically named *Forever*. Because her car—and most likely her body—were going to become one with this godforsaken place. She would become eternally part of Forever's terrain and nobody was even going to realize it because she would live at the bottom of some body of water.

Forever.

Oh, why had she taken this so-called "shortcut"? she upbraided herself. Why hadn't she just gone the long way to Laredo the way she'd initially intended? It wasn't as if she was trying to outdo her brother in trying to land this new account for the family recording label. She was the only one who'd been dispatched to audition the new band The Lonely Wolves. Desperate for their big break, the band would have waited for her to come until hell froze over.

Unfortunately, it wasn't hell freezing over that was

about to be the cause of her demise; it was the torrential rains, all but unheard of in this part of the country at this time of year.

And yet, here it was, a downpour the likes of which she had never witnessed before. The kind that would have had Noah quickly boarding up the door of his ark and nervously setting sail.

The rains had fallen so fast and so heavily, the dry, parched ground—clay for the most part—couldn't begin to absorb it. One minute, she was driving through a basin, her windshield wipers going so fast, she thought they were in danger of just flying off into the wind. The next, the rain was falling so hard that the poor windshield wipers had met their match and did absolutely no good at all.

Stunned, Whitney had done her best, struggling to keep her vehicle straight, all the while getting that sinking feeling that she was fighting a losing battle. Before she knew it, her tires were no longer touching solid ground.

The rains were filling up the basin, turning the cracked, dusty depression into what amounted to a giant container for all this displaced, swiftly accumulating water.

She gave up trying to steer because nothing short of a rudder would have any effect on regaining control of her vehicle. She'd been driving the sports car with the top down and when the rains hit, they came so fast and so heavy, she couldn't get the top to go back up. Now her car swayed and bobbed as well as filled up with water. It didn't take a genius to know what would happen next.

She would be thrown from her car into the swirling waters—which meant that her life was over. She would die flailing frantically in the waters of a miniscule, backwater town.

She wasn't ready to die.

She wasn't!

Whitney opened her mouth to yell for help as loudly as she could. But the second she did, her mouth was immediately filled with water.

Holding on to the sides of the vehicle to steady herself, she tried to yell again. But the car, now at the mercy of the floodwaters, was utterly unsteady. Water was sloshing everywhere. As it crashed against her car, tipping it, Whitney lost her grip.

And then, just like that, she was separated from the vehicle. The forward motion had her all but flying from the car. The next second, she found herself immersed in the dark, swirling waters—waters that hadn't been there a few short heartbeats ago.

Whitney tried desperately to get a second grip on any part of her car, hoping to somehow stay afloat, but the car was sinking.

There was no help coming from anywhere. No one knew she'd taken this shortcut. No one back home really bothered to trace her route—that was partially because she had insisted years ago not to be treated like a child. She could make her own decisions, her own waves, as well. Certainly, at thirty, she was no longer an unsteady child.

So other than competing with her, her siblings—except for Wilson, the oldest—all stayed clear of her, making a point not to get in her way. After all, she *was* the second oldest in the family.

Tears filled Whitney's eyes before the rains could

lash at them. This wasn't how she wanted to die. And certainly not the age she wanted to die, either.

As if she had a choice, the little voice in her head mocked.

Nevertheless, just before she went under, Whitney screamed the word *Help!* again, screamed it as loudly as she could.

She swallowed more water.

And then the waters swallowed her.

Chapter One

The deluge seemed to come out of nowhere.

On his way back to town after a better-than-average rehearsal session with the band he'd helped put together, Liam and the Forever Band, Liam Murphy immediately made his way to high ground at the first sign of a serious rainfall.

Traveling alone out here, the youngest of the Murphy brothers was taking no chances—just in case. Flash floods didn't occur often around here, but they *did* occur and "better safe than sorry" had been a phrase that had been drummed into his head by his older brother Brett from the time he and his other brother Finn had been knee-high to a grasshopper.

As it turned out, Liam had made it to high ground just in time. Rain fell with a vengeance, as if the very sky had been slashed open. As he watched in awed fascination, in less than ten minutes, the onslaught of rain turned the basin below from a virtual dust bowl to a veritable swimming pool—one filled with swirling waters.

More like a whirlpool, Liam silently amended, because the waters were sweeping so angrily over the terrain, mimicking the turbulent waters in a Jacuzzi.

Liam glanced at the clock on his dashboard. Depending on when this was going to let up, he was either going to be late, or *very* late. This, after he'd promised Brett he'd be in to work early. He was due at Murphy's, Forever's only saloon. Fortunately, it belonged to his brothers and him, but Brett was still not going to be happy about this turn of events.

Liam took out his phone, automatically glancing at the upper left-hand corner to see if there were any bars available.

There were.

"Not bad," he murmured to himself when he saw the three small bars. "Service must be improving," he noted with some relief.

There'd been a time, not all that long ago, when no bars were the norm. A few short years ago, the region around Forever, for all intents and purposes, was a dead zone. But progress could only be held off for so long. Civilization had gotten a foothold in the town, though it had to be all but dragged in, kicking and screaming. Even now, on occasion, the strength of the signal was touch and go.

Liam pressed the appropriate buttons. It took a very long minute before the call connected and he could hear the line on the other end ringing. He silently began to count off the number of times the other phone rang.

He was up to four—one more and it went to voice mail—when he heard the cell phone being picked up.

There was an almost deafening crackle and then he heard, "Murphy's."

The deep, baritone voice could only belong to Brett, the oldest Murphy brother, the one who had been responsible for keeping him and Finn from becoming wards of the state when their uncle died a mere eighteen months after both their parents had passed on. Brett had done it at great personal cost, but that was something he and Finn had only found out about years after the fact.

"Brett? It's Liam. Looks like I'm going to be late for my shift," he told his brother. The rain was beating against the rolled-up windows of his truck with a vengeance as if determined to gain access. All that was missing was a big, bad wolf ranting about huffing and puffing.

"Don't tell me, you got caught in this storm."

Liam could hear the concern in his brother's voice—not that Brett would say as much. But it was understood. "Okay, I won't tell you."

He heard Brett sigh. "I always knew you didn't have enough sense to come in out of the rain. Were you at least smart enough to get to high ground?"

"Yes, big brother, the truck and I are on high ground." Even as he said the words, his windows stopped rattling and the rain stopped coming down in buckets. He looked up through the front windshield. It seemed to have stopped coming down at all. "Matter of fact," he said, pausing for a moment as he rolled down the driver's-side window and stuck his hand out, palm up, "I think it just stopped raining."

It never ceased to amaze him just how fast rain seemed to turn itself on and then off again in this part of the country.

"I'd still give it a little time," Brett warned. "In case it starts up again. I'd rather have you late than dead."

Liam laughed shortly. "And on that heartwarming note, I think I'm going to end this call. See you later," he said to his brother. The next moment, Liam hit the glowing red light on his screen, terminating the connection.

Tucking the phone into his back pocket, he continued driving very slowly. As he began guiding his truck back down the incline, he could have sworn he heard a woman's scream.

Liam froze for a second, listening intently.

Nothing.

Had to be one of the ravens, he decided. Most likely a disgruntled bird that hadn't managed to find shelter before the rains hit, although he hadn't seen one just now.

Still, even though he was now driving down the incline to the trail he'd abandoned earlier, Liam kept listening, just to make sure that it was only his imagination—or some wayward animal—that was responsible for the scream he'd thought he'd heard.

If it was his imagination, it was given to re-creating an extremely high-pitched scream, Liam decided, because he'd heard the cry for help again, fainter this time but still urgent, still high—and resoundingly full of absolute terror.

Someone *was* in trouble, Liam thought, searching for the source of the scream.

Throwing caution to the wind, he pushed down on the accelerator. The truck all but danced down the remainder of the incline in what amounted to a jerky motion. He had a death grip on the steering wheel as he proceeded to scan as much of the area around him as humanly possible.

Liam saw that the basin had completely filled up with rainwater. Something like that was enough to compromise any one of a number of people, even those who were familiar with this sort of occurrence and had lived in and around Forever most of their lives.

The water could rush at an unsuspecting driver with the speed of an oncoming train. Sadly, drownings in a flash flood were not unheard of.

With his eyes intently focused, Liam scanned the area again.

And again, he saw nothing except brackish-looking water.

"Maybe it *was* just the wind," Liam murmured under his breath.

He knew that there were times when the wind could sound exactly like a mournful woman pining after a missing lover.

If Brett were here with him, his older brother would have told him to get his tail on home.

Stop letting your imagination run away with you, Brett would have chided.

Liam was just about to get back on the road home when something—a gut feeling, or maybe just some stray, nagging instinct—made him look down into the rushing waters flooding the basin one last time.

That was when he saw her.

Saw the woman.

One minute she wasn't there at all, the next, a half-drowned-looking woman, her shoulder-length brown hair plastered to her face, came shooting up, breaking the water's surface like a man-made geyser, her arms flailing about madly as they came into contact with nothing but the air. It was obvious that she was desperately searching for something solid to grab on to.

The woman was drowning.

He'd only witnessed such abject panic once before in his life. Then it had been on the face of a friend who had accidentally discharged a pistol and missed his head by an inch, or less. The horror of what could have happened had been visible in his friend's shaken expression.

This time the horror of what could be was on the face of an angel. A very desperate, panicky, wet angel.

Before he had time to assess if this waterlogged angel was real or a mere figment of his overactive, overwrought imagination, Liam leaped out of his truck and came flying down the rest of the incline. There was no time to think, to evaluate and make calculated decisions. There was only time to act and act quickly.

Which he did.

Without pausing, he flung off his jacket because it would keep his arms too confined and from the little he had time to assess, he was going to need all the upper-arm power he could manage to summon. Leaving on his boots and hat, Liam dived into the water.

SHE WAS GOING DOWN for the last time.

Four, she'd counted four. Four times she'd gone down and managed to somehow get back up again, desperately gasping for air.

Her thoughts were colliding wildly with one another. And she was hallucinating, Whitney was sure of it, because she'd just seen someone plunging into the water to rescue her.

Except that he wasn't real. This area was deserted. There was no one around, no one to rescue her.

She was going to die.

Suddenly, Whitney thought she felt something. Or

was that someone? Whatever it was, it was grabbing her by the arm, no, wait, by the waist. Was she being pulled up, out of the homicidal waters?

No, it wasn't possible.

Wasn't possible.

It was just her mind giving her something to hang on to before life finally, irrevocably drained out of her forever.

Just a figment of her imagination. This rescuing hero she'd conjured up, he wasn't real.

And very, very soon, Whitney knew she wouldn't be real, either. But right now, she could have sworn she was being roughly dragged up out of the water.

Where was the light? Wasn't she supposed to be going toward some kind of light? Whitney wondered. But there was no light, there was only pressure and pain and the sound of yelling.

Did they yell in heaven?

Or was this the Other Place? She hadn't been an angel, but she wasn't bad enough to land in hell.

Was she?

But being sent to hell would explain why something was beating against her, pushing on her ribs over and over again.

"C'MON, DAMN IT, breathe! Breathe!" Liam ordered, frustrated and fearful all at the same time. The woman wasn't responding.

Damn it, Brett was the one who should be here, not him, Liam thought as he continued with his chest compressions. Brett would know what to do to save this woman. He just remembered bits and pieces of CPR, not from any sort of training but from programs he'd watched on TV as a kid.

Still, it was the only thing he could think to do and it was better than standing helplessly by, watching this woman die in front of him.

So he continued, almost on automatic pilot. Ten compressions against the chest, then mouth to mouth, and then back to compressions again until the dead were brought back to life.

Except that this woman—whoever she was—wasn't responding.

He was losing her.

The thought made him really angry and he worked harder.

Liam began another round, moving faster, pushing harder this time. He fully intended on continuing in this manner until he got some sort of a response from the woman he'd rescued from the water. Granted she'd looked more dead than alive when he'd pulled her out, but when he put his head against her chest, he was positive that he'd detected just the faintest sound of a heartbeat.

It gave him just a sliver of hope and he intended to build on that.

IT CAME TO HER in a blurred, painful haze: she wasn't dead.

Dead people didn't hurt.

Did they?

Whitney hadn't given much thought to reaching the afterlife. She'd always been far too preoccupied in getting ahead in the life that she had on earth. But she felt fairly certain that after transitioning to the afterlife, pain and discomfort were no longer involved, certainly not to this degree—and she was definitely experiencing both.

Big-time.

After what seemed like an absolute eternity, Whitney came to the realization that she wasn't inside of some dark abyss—or hell. The problem was that her eyes were shut. Not simply shut, it felt more as if they were glued down that way.

With what felt like almost superhuman effort, she kept on struggling until she finally managed to pry her eyes open.

Focusing took another full minute—her surroundings were a complete blur at first, wavy lines that made no sense. Part of her was convinced that she was still submerged.

But that was air she was taking in, not water, so she couldn't be underwater any longer. And what was that odd, heavy pain across her chest that she kept feeling almost rhythmically?

And then she saw him.

Saw a man with wet, medium blond hair just inches away from her face—and he had his hands crisscrossed on top of her chest.

"Why…are…you…pushing…on…my…chest?" The raspy words felt as if they had dragged themselves up a throat that was lined with jagged pieces of glass.

They weren't any louder than a faint whisper.

Liam's head jerked up and he almost lost his balance, certainly his count. Stunned, he stared at her in surprise and disbelief.

It worked! he thought, silently congratulating himself. She was alive!

He'd saved a life!

"I'm giving you CPR," he told her. "And I guess it worked," he added with pride and no small sense of satisfaction. He felt almost light-headed from his success.

"Then…I'm…not…dead?" she asked uncertainly. It took Whitney a second to process this influx of information on the heels of the panic that had enveloped her.

The last thing she clearly remembered was being thrown from the car and sinking into dirty water.

"Not unless I am, too—and I wasn't when I last checked," he told her. He'd actually saved a life. How about that? Right now, Liam felt as if he could walk on water.

It took him a minute to get back to reality.

The woman he'd rescued was looking at him with the widest green eyes he'd ever seen. She tried to sit up only to have him push her back down again. Confused, disoriented, she looked at him uncertainly.

"I don't think you should sit up just yet," he told her. She wanted to argue with him, but the energy just wasn't there. "You almost drowned. Why don't you give yourself a couple of minutes to recover?" he suggested tactfully.

"I'm…fine…" she insisted.

She certainly *was* fine, Liam couldn't help thinking. Even looking like a partially drowned little rabbit, there was no denying that this woman was strikingly beautiful. No amount of wet, slicked-back hair could change that.

Still, Liam didn't want her trying to run off just yet. She could collapse and hit her head—or worse. He hadn't just risked his own life to pull her out of the rushing waters only to have her bring about her own demise.

He continued to restrain her very gently.

"I just saved your life," Liam told her patiently. "Humor me."

The rains had obviously stopped and the waters, even now, were trying, ever so slowly, to recede. Within a couple of hours or so, it would be as if this had never happened—except that it had and an out-of-towner had almost died in it.

Talk about being in the right place at the right time, he mused. He was grateful now that band practice had run a little over. If it hadn't, he would have passed the basin when the rains hit and he would have never been there to rescue this woman.

"Okay." Whitney gave in, partially because she felt about as weak as a day-old kitten and partially because she was trying to humor the cowboy who had apparently rescued her. "But just for a few minutes," she stipulated, her speech still a little slow, definitely not as animated as it normally was.

Whitney tried to move her shoulders and got nowhere. Whoever this man was, he was strong. Definitely stronger than she was, she thought.

She'd never trusted strangers—but this one had saved her life so maybe a little trust *was* in order.

"Does this kind of thing happen often?" Whitney asked warily. Because if it did, she couldn't understand why anyone would want to live here.

Why not? her inner voice mocked. *You live in the land of earthquakes. One natural disaster is pretty much like another.*

Her expression remained stony as she waited for the cowboy to give her an answer.

"No, not often," Liam assured her, removing his hands from her shoulders. "But when it does, I guarantee that it leaves one hell of an impression."

The woman was trying to sit up again, he realized. Rather than watch her digging her elbows into the ground to try to push herself up, Liam put his hands back on her shoulders, exerting just the right amount of pressure to keep her down.

The look she gave him was a mixture of exasperation and confusion.

"Why don't you just hold on to me and I'll get you into a sitting position," Liam suggested.

Having no choice—she was *not* in any shape to outwrestle him and she suspected that out-arguing this gentle-spoken cowboy might be harder than it appeared—Whitney did as he proposed.

With her arms wrapped around his neck, Whitney was slowly raised into a sitting position. She realized that she was just a few feet away from what had been angry, dangerous waters a very short time ago, not to mention her final resting place.

The scene registered for the first time. The man beside her had risked his life to save hers. Why?

"You dived into that?" she asked in semi-disbelief.

Liam nodded. "I had to," he replied simply. "You weren't about to walk on water and come out on your own. What happened?" he asked. "Did the water overwhelm you?" Then, before she could answer, he added another basic question to the growing stack in his head. "Why weren't you swimming?"

She was about to lie, saying whatever excuse came

to mind, but then she stopped herself. This man had risked his life in order to save her. She owed him the truth.

"I don't know how," she murmured almost under her breath.

Liam stared at her, still not 100 percent convinced. "Really?"

Her very last ounce of energy had been summarily depleted as she had devoted every single ounce within her to staying alive in the swiftly moving waters. If it hadn't been, she would have been annoyed at his display of disbelief.

"Really," she answered wearily.

"Never met anyone who didn't know how to swim," he commented.

"Well, now you have," she answered, trying her best to come around enough to stand up.

Since the torrents had abated and she was now sitting on the ground, utterly soaked, Whitney looked around the immediate area.

That's when it finally hit her. She wasn't overlooking it. It wasn't anywhere in sight.

"Where's my car?" she asked the man who had rescued her.

Liam looked at her a touch uncertainly.

"What car?"

Chapter Two

"What do you mean 'What car?'" Whitney asked, bewildered as she echoed her rescuer's words back to him. "*My* car."

The events of the past few minutes were far from crystal clear in her mind, however, amid the lashing rains and the tumultuous rising waters in the basin, Whitney was fairly certain that her car hadn't sunk to the bottom of the threatening waters. She and the car had gone their separate ways, but she was sure that she'd been thrown from the vehicle as it was raised up, not pushed down.

Liam shook his head. "I didn't see any car," he told her honestly. "All I saw was you."

"But I was in a car," she insisted. "At least, I think I was." She looked at him, struggling to keep her disorientation and mounting panic contained. "How do you think I got out here?"

Liam had done very little thinking in the past few minutes, mostly reacting. He was still reacting right now. Saving a life was a heady feeling and it certainly didn't hurt matters that she was a knockout, even soaking wet.

He shrugged in response to her question and hazarded a guess, his expression giving nothing away.

"Divine intervention?" It was half a question, half an answer.

"No, I was driving a car," Whitney retorted, then took a breath. Her nerves felt as if they were systematically being shredded. "A pearl-white Mercedes," she described. There couldn't be any other cars like that around, she reasoned, not in a town that was hardly larger than a puddle. "A sports car," she elaborated. "I wound up being thrown from my car because I couldn't get the top up once that awful deluge started. Don't you people get weather warnings?" she asked, frustrated. She'd always been in control of a situation and what she'd just been through had taken that away from her.

She didn't like feeling this way.

"Sometimes," Liam answered, although he had a feeling that wouldn't have done her any good. The woman would have had to have her radio station set to local news and he had a hunch she would have been listening to some hard-rock singer.

Her story about being thrown from her vehicle was completely plausible. There was no way she would have been out here without a car or at least *some* mode of transportation.

But if that was the case, where was her car? Had it gotten completely filled with rainwater and wound up submerged? If so, it would turn up once the floodwaters receded. Unless the turbulent basin waters had succeeded in dragging it out to the gulf.

In either case, the car she was asking about wasn't anywhere to be seen.

Just for good measure, and because the woman appeared so utterly distraught, Liam looked around the surrounding area again.

Slowly.

Which was when he saw it.

Saw the car the woman had to be asking about. The topless white vehicle wasn't lying mangled on the side of the newly created bank, but it might as well have been for all the use she could get out of it in its present position.

How was she going to take this latest twist? he couldn't help wondering.

Only one way to find out, Liam decided, bracing himself. "Is that your car?" he asked, pointing toward the only vehicle—besides his own—in their vicinity.

Hope sprang up within her as Whitney looked around. But she didn't see anything that even resembled her gleaming white vehicle—

Until she did.

Whitney wasn't aware of her mouth dropping open as she rose to her feet and walked toward her car, moving like someone in a trance—or more accurately, in a very bad dream.

"Yes." Her voice was barely a whisper and she felt numb all over as she stared at the Mercedes in utter disbelief. Her beautiful white vehicle appeared to be relatively intact—but there was one major problem with it.

The white sports car was caught up in a tree.

"What's it doing up there?" she cried, her voice cracking at the end of her question.

None of this seemed real to her, not the sudden deluge coming out of nowhere, not the fact that she had almost drowned in water that hadn't been there minutes earlier and certainly not the fact that her car now had an aerial view of the area.

"By the looks of it, I'd say hanging," Liam replied quietly.

"Can't you get it down?" she asked him. She hadn't the faintest idea on how to proceed from here if he gave her a negative answer.

As she looked up at him hopefully, Liam gave her a crooked grin. "I might be strong," he told her, "but I'm not *that* strong." Having said that, Liam took out his cell phone. Within a second, his fingers were tapping out a number on his keypad.

"Are you calling AAA?" she asked.

Again, Liam smiled. He was calling the only one everyone in the area called when they had car trouble, Forever's best—and only—mechanic.

"I'm calling Mick," he told her. "He might be rated AAA, I don't know, but he's been a car mechanic for as long as I've known him and he's pretty much seen everything."

Maybe it was because her brain was somewhat addled from its underwater adventure, but the fact that this cowboy was calling some hayseed mechanic didn't exactly fill her with confidence or sound overly encouraging to her.

Whitney took a step closer to the tree and to her dismay, she realized that she'd lost one of her shoes during her brief nonswim. That left her very lopsided. The fact only registered as she found herself pitching forward.

The upshot of that was she would have been communing—face-first—with the wet ground if the man who had initially pulled her out of the water hadn't lunged and made a grab for her now, grabbing her by the waist.

"Are you okay?" Liam wanted to know, doing his own quick once-over of the woman—just in case. His arm stayed where it was, around her waist.

She wanted to say yes, she was fine. She'd been trained to say yes and then pull back, so that she could go back to managing on her own. But training or not, she still felt rather shaky inside, the way a person who had just come face-to-face with their own mortality might.

Given that state of mind, in a moment of weakness, Whitney answered him truthfully, "I don't know yet."

Turning so that he was facing her *and* the incline, he indicated his truck. "Why don't you sit down in the cab of my truck while we wait for Mick to get here? Or, better yet, I could take you to the clinic in town if you want to be checked out."

"Clinic?" she repeated with a slight bewildered frown. "You mean hospital, right?"

"No, I mean clinic," he replied. "If you want a hospital, I could take you," he said, then warned her, "but the closest one is approximately fifty miles away in Pine Ridge."

He was kidding, right? Were the hospitals around here really *that* far apart?

"Fifty miles away?" Whitney echoed, utterly stunned. "What if there's a medical emergency?" she asked.

Fortunately, they had that covered now—but it hadn't always been that way. The residents of Forever had gone some thirty years between doctors until Dan Davenport had come to fill the vast vacancy.

"It would have to be a pretty big emergency to be

something that Dr. Dan and Lady Doc couldn't handle," Liam told her.

Very gently, he tried to guide her over to his truck, but the petite woman firmly held her ground. She had to be stronger than she looked.

Dr. Dan. Lady Doc. She felt like Alice after the fictional character had slid down the rabbit hole. For a second, Whitney thought that the cowboy was putting her on, but there wasn't even a hint of a smile curving his rather sensual mouth and not so much as a glimmer of humor in his eyes.

He was serious.

What kind of a place *was* this?

"So, do you want to go?" Liam prodded.

"Go? Go where?" Whitney asked. Her light eyebrows came together in what looked like an upside-down *V*.

"To the clinic," Liam repeated patiently. If she couldn't keep abreast of the conversation, maybe he *should* just take her to the clinic even if she didn't want to go. He sincerely doubted that she could offer any real resistance if he decided to load her into his truck and drive into town. And it would be for her own good.

"No, I'm okay," Whitney insisted. "A little rattled, but I'm okay," she repeated with more conviction. "And I'll be more okay when my car is taken down out of that tree."

Looking over her shoulder to see if she had finally convinced him, she found that the cowboy had walked away from her. The next moment, he was back. He had a fleece-lined denim jacket in his hand that he then proceeded to drape over her shoulders.

"You look cold," he explained when she looked at

him warily. "And you're already chilled. Thought this might help."

Her natural inclination to argue subsided in the face of this new display of thoughtfulness. Besides, she had begun to feel a cold chill corkscrewing down along her spine. The jacket was soft and warm and given half a chance, she would have just curled up in it and gone to sleep. She was exhausted. The next moment, she was fighting that feeling.

Whitney smiled at the cowboy and said, "Thank you."

"Don't mention it," he responded, then extended his hand to her. "I'm Liam, by the way. Liam Murphy."

Whitney slipped her hand into his, absently noting how strong it felt as she shook it. "Whitney Marlowe," she responded.

Liam's grin widened. "Pleased to meet you, Whitney Marlowe," he said, then added, "Sorry the circumstances weren't better."

Whitney laughed softly to herself. "They could have been worse," she told him. When he looked at her quizzically, she explained, "You might not have heard me in time and then I would have drowned."

What she said was true, but he had learned a long time ago not to focus on the bad, only the good. "Not a pretty picture to dwell on," he said.

"Nonetheless, I owe you my life."

The grin on his face widened considerably. If she really felt that way, he could take it a step further. "You know, in some corners of the world, that would mean that your life is now mine."

"Oh?" The single word was wrapped in wariness. "But this isn't 'some corner of the world.' This is

Texas," she pointed out. "And people don't own other people here anymore and haven't for a very long time," she added just in case he was getting any funny ideas.

He could almost *feel* her tension escalating. "Relax," he soothed her in a calming voice that, judging by her expression, just irritated her more. "It's just a saying. You sure you don't want me taking you into town so you can get checked out at the clinic?"

"I'm sure," she insisted as adamantly as she could, given the circumstances. Her throat felt as if she'd swallowed a frog wearing pointy stilettos that scraped across her throat with every word she uttered.

The noise she heard coming in the distance alerted her of the car mechanic's impending arrival.

Whitney turned toward the sound and if she'd been expecting a large, souped-up-looking tow truck, she was sadly disappointed. Mick, the town mechanic who had been summoned to the scene, was driving a beat-up twenty-year-old truck that had definitely seen far better days.

Stopping his truck directly opposite Liam's, Mick lumbered out. Thin, he still had the gait and stride of a man who had once been a great deal heavier than the shadow he cast now.

Mick took out his bandanna-like handkerchief and wiped his brow, then passed it over his graying, perpetual two-day-old stubble.

"What can I do you for, Little Murphy?" he asked Liam, tucking the bandanna back in his pocket.

Putting one hand on Mick's sloping shoulder, Liam directed the man's attention to the reason he had been called. "Lady got her car stuck in that tree."

"And you want me to get it down," Mick guessed.

Taking off his cap, he scratched his bald head as he took a couple of steps closer to the tree.

"That's the general idea," Liam replied.

Mick nodded his head. "And a good one, too," he commented seriously, "except for one thing."

"What's that?" Whitney asked, cutting in. She didn't like being ignored and left out of the conversation. After all, it *was* her car up there.

"The thing of it is," Mick told her honestly, "I don't have anything I can use to get that car down." He squinted, continuing to look at the car. "I could cut the tree down," he offered. "That would get the car down, but I sure couldn't guarantee its condition once it hit the ground again." His brown eyes darted toward Liam. "You're going to need something a lot more flexible than my old truck for this."

"So what do I do?" Whitney asked. This was a nightmare. A genuine nightmare.

"Beats me," Mick said in all honesty.

Liam suddenly had an idea. "Would a cherry picker work?"

Mick bit the inside of his cheek, a clear sign that he was thinking the question over. "It might," he said. "But where are you gonna get one of those?"

"From Connie," Liam replied, brightening up. Why hadn't he thought of this before? he silently demanded. It seemed like the perfect solution to the problem.

"Who's Connie?" Whitney asked, unwilling to be left on the sidelines again. She looked from Liam to the mechanic.

"Finn's fiancée," Liam answered, clearly excited about this new solution he'd just come up with. Taking out his cell phone again, he made another call.

Connie, Finn, Mick. It sounded like a cast of characters in a strange college revue, Whitney thought. How did *any* of this get her reunited with her car? she wondered impatiently.

Because the man who rescued her from a watery grave was on the phone, she glanced at the scruffy man in coveralls whom Liam had called to the scene first. "Who's Finn?" she asked.

"That's Liam's brother. One of them, anyway," Mick amended.

"And this Finn, his fiancée has a cherry picker?" Whitney asked incredulously. This definitely sounded surreal to her. What kind of woman had a cherry picker on her property? And what would she be doing with one, anyway?

"She does," Mick confirmed.

It still sounded unbelievable to her. Whitney waited for more of an explanation. When none came, she realized she hadn't gone about this the right way. She had to ask for an explanation before she could expect one to be forthcoming. Even that struck her as strange. Didn't these people like to spin tall tales, or go endlessly on and on about things?

So why did she have to pull everything out of them? "*Why* does she have a cherry picker?" Whitney asked.

Liam had quickly placed and completed his call. Tucking his phone away, he answered her question for her before Mick could. "Because Connie's in the construction business and she's currently building Forever's first hotel."

Something was *finally* making sense, Whitney thought with relief. "And she's willing to let you borrow it?"

"Better than that," Liam told her. "She's willing to

have one of her crew drive it over here and get your car down," he corrected.

Liam took no offense at the extra measure. He was actually relieved about it. Intrigued though he was about getting a chance to handle a cherry picker, this was really not the time for him to get a new experience under his belt. Especially if he wound up dropping the very thing he was attempting to rescue.

Besides, he'd already had his new experience for the day—he had never saved a person's life before and even though he had expertly deflected compliments and thanks, knowing that he had saved a life still generated a radiant feeling within him.

Having answered Whitney's question, he turned toward Mick and asked the mechanic, "Are you going to stick around?"

Mick nodded his head.

"The car might need a little babying once it's on flat ground." He gestured toward the white car. "Those kind of vehicles really thrive on attention."

Whitney frowned. "You're talking about my car like it's a person."

Mick obviously saw no reason to contradict her. "Yes, ma'am, I am. And it is," the mechanic assured her. "And it's a she, not a he. It responds to a soft touch and kindness much better than to a rough hand," he explained, making his case.

Whitney opened her mouth to protest and argue the point. She had every intention on setting the grizzled old man straight.

But then she shut her mouth again, deciding that it really wasn't worth the effort. This wasn't the big city and people thought differently out here in the sticks.

The mechanic seemed cantankerous and if she had a guess, she would have said that the man was extremely set in his ways—as was his right, she supposed.

When she got down to it, as long as this mechanic got her car down out of the tree and running, what he called the car or how he interacted with it really didn't matter all that much.

"What are you doing here?" Liam asked her, averting what he took to be a budding clash of wills.

Whitney turned around to look at the cowboy. The question, coming out of the blue, caught her off guard. "What?"

"What are you doing here?" Liam repeated. "In Forever," he added in case she didn't understand his question.

Whitney laughed shortly. "You mean when I'm not drowning in a flash flood?"

Liam's easy grin materialized again. "Yeah, when you're not doing that. What brought you to Forever? Are you visiting someone?"

As a rule, they didn't get many people traveling to Forever—unless they were visiting a relative and Liam was fairly certain that if this woman was related to anyone in town, he would have known about it.

Still, in the past couple of years, they'd had people coming to the town and making changes to the structure of Forever's very way of life.

"Nothing," Whitney told him. "I was just on my way to Laredo."

"Laredo?" He rolled the name over in his head, mentally pinpointing the city on a map. "That's kind of out of your way, isn't it?" Liam asked.

She didn't like being wrong. Having that pointed

out to her was a pet peeve of hers and she had trouble ignoring it. "I was just following the map—"

"Guess your map's wrong, then," Liam informed her simply.

"I'm beginning to get that impression," she answered with a barely suppressed sigh.

Chapter Three

"Now, there's something you don't see every day," Mick commented.

Before either Liam or Whitney could ask what he was referring to, the mechanic pointed behind them. Turning, they saw a bright orange cherry picker being driven straight toward them.

Maybe this was going to turn out all right after all, Whitney thought.

"Somebody put out a call for a cherry picker?" the machine's operator, Henry MacKenzie, asked cheerfully as he climbed down from inside the cab. He approached Liam, obviously assuming that he was the one in charge. "Ms. Carmichael told me to tell you that this baby is at your disposal for as long as you need it. I guess, by association, I am, too. Unless you know how to operate this thing and want to do the honors yourself," the tall, burly man added.

Henry, along with several others on the construction crew, had initially been sent out from Houston by the construction company's business manager, Stewart Emerson. Highly skilled laborers, they were needed to operate the machinery that had been shipped out to do the basic foundation work for Forever's first hotel.

At this point, that part of the project had been finished more than a month ago, but the men—and their machines—had been instructed to remain on-site until the project was completed. Emerson had paid them well to remain in Forever and on call—just in case some unforeseen glitch suddenly made their services necessary.

Eager though he might have been to try his hand at operating the fancy forklift's controls, Liam had no desire to risk retrieving the car from out of the tree merely to satisfy his own curiosity. One wrong move on his part and the car was liable to become a thousand-piece puzzle.

He definitely didn't want to be the one responsible for that unfortunate turn of events.

"No, haven't got a clue," Liam confessed. "She's all yours."

Henry nodded his head, clearly expecting the reply he'd just heard.

"So why do you think you need a cherry picker way out here?" Henry asked. He looked from Liam to Mick and then to Whitney.

"Because of that," Liam answered, pointing to one of the trees along the basin.

"That tree?" Henry asked. "Why would you— Oh." The cherry picker's operator stopped abruptly as he took in the entire scene and finally saw the precariously perched vehicle. He laughed shortly as he shook his head in wonder. "You people sure don't make things easy out here, do you?"

Anxious about the condition of her sports car, Whitney cut to the chase. "Do you think you can get it down?" she asked.

"Oh, I can get it down, all right. But it's not going

to be easy and it's not going to be fast," Henry warned. "And it might not even be in one piece. But I can get it down," he reasoned.

Getting the car piecemeal wasn't going to do her any good. "How long would it take you if you took the proper precautions to get it down in one piece?" Whitney asked.

"Won't know until I start," Henry answered. "I'm also going to have to have someone working with me," he added, giving the situation further thought. "This is *not* a one-man job."

"What do you need?" Liam asked.

"I need someone in the basket," Henry said, nodding at the extreme upper part of the cherry picker. "To secure the car," he explained. "Otherwise, the damn thing'll just come crashing down to the ground the second we try to move it."

"Tell me what to do," Liam told the operator, volunteering for the job.

Henry laughed softly to himself. "The first thing you need to do is back away from the cherry picker and let me call someone on-site," the man said seriously. "No offense—and thanks for the offer—but this'll go a whole lot better and faster if someone with experience is doing it."

Liam took no offense at being turned down. "I get it. But in the interest of time, I thought I'd volunteer." And then he felt compelled to add, "Securing a car isn't rocket science."

"Might not be rocket science," Henry agreed, "but one wrong move and no car, either. Hey, it don't matter to me one way or the other, but I think this little lady might have something to say about it." Henry's small, deep-set brown eyes darted toward her.

Whitney was still having trouble wrapping her mind around this rather strange turn of events: first she nearly drowned, and then her vehicle was thrown into a tree. It all felt like some sort of a bizarre nightmare. A small part of Whitney thought that she'd actually wake up at any moment.

The more practical side of her, however, knew that was not about to happen. Her car really *was* stuck in a tree—and would remain there unless drastic measures were taken.

"Do whatever it takes," Whitney told the machine operator.

"Yes, ma'am," Henry replied. He was on his cell phone in less than five seconds, calling for one of the other crew members to come out. "Need a hand here, Rick," he said to the man who had answered his call. "You're not going to believe this," he added with a deep chuckle. "No, I'm not going to tell you. This you've got to come out and see for yourself. Boss lady okayed this job," he added in case there were any questions about priorities. Henry rattled off the same directions to Rick that he had been given earlier.

With that part of it taken care of, Liam turned his attention to Mick. "Looks like it's going to be a while before they have the car on solid ground," Liam told the mechanic. "Why don't you go back to the shop? I can call you once the car's ready to be looked over," Liam suggested.

Mick raised his rather wide shoulders and then let them drop again in a dismissive shrug. "Ain't got no other place to be right now," he confessed. "Mrs. Abernathy took her old Buick last night so there's nothing for me to work on in the shop. I might as well stay here and watch history being made," Mick said philosophically, his eyes all but glowing with fascination as he stared up at the treed vehicle.

"Suit yourself," Liam said. "You don't mind if I take her to the diner to get a bite to eat, do you?" he asked, indicating Whitney. Since he was the one who had put in the call to Mick in the first place, he felt a little guilty about leaving the man here more or less on call.

"Not as long as you bring me back somethin'," Mick qualified.

"Like what?"

Mick began to slowly circle the tree, searching for the path of least resistance. "Surprise me," Mick answered.

Having been privy to the entire exchange, Whitney frowned—deeply. Granted there was a part of her that longed for a strong, forceful man to take charge. However, the greater part of Whitney was wary of someone usurping her control over her life and that was exactly the part that was presently balking at what Liam had just told his mechanic friend.

"What if I don't want to go for 'a bite'?" Whitney asked.

"I'm not about to force-feed you, if that's what you're worried about," Liam said, then asked, "You're not hungry?"

She wanted to say no, she wasn't. The problem was that she *was* hungry. Very.

As if to bear witness to that, her stomach suddenly rumbled—not quietly but all too loudly.

"If you're not hungry," Liam continued, "I think

you should tell your stomach because I get the definite impression that your stomach seems to think it's *very* hungry."

She lifted one shoulder in a disinterested shrug. The jacket began to slip off and she made a grab for it, returning it to its place.

"I suppose it can't hurt to go get something to eat," she allowed.

"Well, maybe in some cases," Liam told her in all honesty, "but not when it involves Miss Joan."

Following him to where he had parked his truck, Whitney stopped walking and took hold of his elbow, turning him around to face her.

"Wait, are you taking me to someone's house?" she asked, ready to put the skids on this venture before it got underway. She was in no mood to be friendly and exchange small talk with some stranger bearing the quaint name of "Miss Joan." Right now, she wasn't up to exchanging discomfort for a hot meal.

"No, we're not going to someone's house," Liam assured her. "Although she's there so much, there are times I think that the diner really could double for her home."

Her head hurt and all these details that Liam kept tossing out were just making it that much worse. "'She,' who's this 'she' you're referring to?" Whitney asked.

A control freak for most of her life—she no longer saw the point in disputing her siblings' accusations—it was hard for her to just hand over the reins to someone in matters that concerned her. But she had no idea when this person the cherry picker operator had called was going to get there. And she *was* hungry.

She supposed there was no harm in going along with

this wandering Good Samaritan, she thought, slanting a look in Liam's direction—at least until her car was back on solid ground.

"Miss Joan," Liam said, answering her question. "She's the 'she' I was referring to. It's her diner."

"Oh."

The pieces started to fall into place, making some sort of sense. She supposed she was being too edgy. Whenever she felt the slightest bit insecure, she could be demanding, needing to know every detail of the future. This man who had rescued her—and was now trying to rescue her car—didn't deserve to have her constantly challenging his every move.

"All right. As long as I get a call the minute my car is down and ready to go," Whitney ordered. She was looking directly at Henry when she said it.

"You heard the lady," Liam said, eyeing Mick. "Do me a favor and call me on my cell."

"You got it," Mick replied, then promised, "The second it's down, I'll give you a call."

Henry nodded his agreement.

At which point Liam regarded Whitney. "Good enough?" he asked her.

It would have to be, Whitney decided.

"Let's go," she told Liam just as her stomach offered up another symphony of off-key, embarrassing growling noises.

Liam brought her over to his truck, opened the passenger door and stood by it, waiting for her to get in.

"Are you planning on strapping me in, too?" Whitney asked, wondering why he was just standing there like that instead of getting in on the driver's side.

He grinned. "Just want to make sure you don't need any help getting in," he explained.

Buckling up, Whitney flashed him a look of irritation. "Why, do I look feeble to you? I've been getting into cars and sitting down rather successfully for more than a couple of decades now."

He answered her truthfully. "You don't look feeble but you do look pale."

The last thing she needed was to be criticized by a cowboy.

"Good," Whitney quipped. "I was going for a pale look," she told him flippantly.

"Then I guess you've succeeded." Liam started up his truck, then rolled down the window on his side before putting the truck into Drive. As he drove past Henry and Mick, he called out, "I'll be back soon."

Both men nodded in acknowledgment.

With that, Liam drove toward town.

THERE WAS SILENCE for the first few minutes of the drive. Not the comfortable kind of silence that two people who ended each other's sentences might have slipped into, but the awkward kind of silence that became steadily deeper and more ominous as the seconds ticked into minutes, then hung around oppressively.

Enduring it for as long as possible, Liam decided that enough was enough.

"You always have this chip on your shoulder, or is this something new for you?" he asked Whitney.

"I don't have a chip," she informed Liam indignantly, sitting up stiffly as her entire body became completely rigid.

"Yes, you do," Liam contradicted. "From where I'm

sitting, that chip is pretty damn big and very nearly impenetrable. In case you haven't noticed, these people are just trying to help you."

"I noticed," she said a bit too defensively.

Whitney paused, pressing her lips together. She was searching for a way to get her point across without sounding as if she had an ax to grind. She really didn't; it was just that because of this setback, she had gone into overdrive. Whenever that happened, she wound up having the kind of personality that put people off. All except for the people she signed to recording contracts. That group would have been willing to cut the devil some slack as long as they got what they were after: a shot at the big time. And because of what she did for a living and the label she was associated with, she was their first step in the right direction.

"But they're not trying to help me out of the goodness of their hearts, it's just business. Everyone's going to get paid for their services," she told Liam, wondering why he thought that was so altruistic.

"Mick's hanging around, waiting for your car to be brought down from its perch. A savvy businessman would have gone back to the shop—and charged you just for coming out," Liam pointed out.

"This way he gets to charge me for his downtime," she countered.

Liam shook his head. "That's not the way Mick operates," he disagreed, then said with emphasis, "That's not how any of us operate around here."

She wasn't ready to believe that. After all, this was just some tiny Texas town, not Oz. However, in the interest of not starting an argument, she merely said, "If you say so."

"I do, but that doesn't mean anything. I guess you'll just have to see for yourself. There it is," he said abruptly.

She sat up a little straighter, as if she'd just been put on notice.

"There 'what' is?" Whitney asked, her green eyes sweeping up and down the muddy road ahead of her. From where she was sitting, it just looked like open country—and more of the same.

"Miss Joan's," Liam elaborated, gesturing up ahead and to the left.

As Whitney looked, the diner came into view more clearly. It looked like a long, silver tube on wheels and it was completely unimpressive in her opinion.

It was also rather blinding.

The sun, which had decided to come out in full regalia now that all the water had been purged out of the sky, seemed to be literally bouncing off the sides of the diner. It made it rather difficult to see, if anyone wanted to drive past the establishment.

But Liam had no intentions of driving past the diner. For him, the diner was journey's end.

He pulled his truck up to the informal area that was the diner's unofficial parking lot.

When Liam turned off the engine, she looked at him. The diner made her think of a third-rate, greasy-spoon establishment that played fast and loose with sanitary conditions. It definitely didn't inspire confidence.

"Isn't there another restaurant we could go to?" she asked as he began to open the door on his side.

Liam paused, his hand on the door handle. "Not without driving fifty miles."

There it was again, she thought. That fifty-mile

separation from everything civilized. Was everything of any worth in this region automatically fifty miles away?

Whitney looked grudgingly at the diner. Maybe she would be lucky and not get ptomaine poisoning.

"Seems to me that this town would do a whole lot better if it just picked itself up and moved fifty miles away," she said cynically.

"We like Forever just where it is and the way it is," Liam informed her.

Yeah, backward and hopelessly behind the times, she thought to herself. Out loud, Whitney offered up another, less hostile description. "Old-fashioned and impossibly quaint?"

"Honest and straightforward," he contradicted.

"Well, I guess that really puts me in my place," she quipped.

He laughed, shaking his head. "I really doubt if anything could ever put you in your place—unless you wanted to be there," he qualified.

Getting out of his truck, he rounded the hood and came around to her side. Opening the door for Whitney, he put his hand out as if to help her get out.

She looked down at it for a moment as if debating whether or not she should take it. Deciding that it wouldn't hurt anything to act graciously, she wrapped her fingers around his.

"I'm sorry," she told him.

He looked surprised by this unusual turn of events. "For?"

In for a penny, in for a pound. Wasn't that what her mother used to say before she ran off? Whitney decided that she might as well say it.

"For acting like an ungrateful brat." She flushed as her own label hit home. "I guess I'm a little out of my element. I'm usually the one on the receiving end of gratitude, not on the giving side."

He wasn't exactly sure what she was trying to say, but he knew contrition when he saw it and he had never been the kind who enjoyed making people squirm. "Hey, you just went through a harrowing experience. You're allowed to act out a little."

His forgiving attitude made her feel even guiltier than she already did.

Their hands were still linked and he tugged on hers just a little. "C'mon," he coaxed. "Everything will seem a lot better after you eat something. Angel will whip up something that'll make you feel as if you've died and gone to heaven."

"Angel?" she repeated a little uncertainly.

"Miss Joan's head cook. Woman could make a mud pie taste appetizing," he told her with enthusiasm.

"I think I'll pass on the mud pie, but I could go for a cheeseburger and fries."

"Great," he responded, drawing her into the diner. "Get ready to have the best cheeseburger and fries you've ever had."

She sincerely doubted that, but she decided to play along. After all, she owed him.

Chapter Four

"So this is the little lady you saved from a watery grave, eh?"

The rather unusual greeting came from Miss Joan less than a heartbeat after Liam had walked into the diner with Whitney at his side.

As was her habit, Miss Joan, ever on top of things, seemed to appear out of nowhere and was right next to them.

Amber eyes took measure of the young stranger quickly, sweeping over her from top to toe in record time, even for Miss Joan. She noted that the young woman was struggling very hard to keep from trembling. *Small wonder,* Miss Joan assessed.

"You look pretty good for someone who'd just cheated death less than a few hours ago. Wet, but good," she amended for the sake of precision.

Stunned, Whitney held on to the ends of the sheepskin jacket, unconsciously using it as a barrier between herself and the older woman. She slanted an uneasy look at Liam.

"Did you just call and tell her about the flash flood—and everything?" she added vaguely. How else could the woman have known that she almost drowned unless Liam had told her?

"Nobody has to call and tell Miss Joan anything," Liam assured her. "She's always just seemed to *know* things, usually right after they happen."

"How?" Whitney asked. Did the woman claim to be clairvoyant?

The smile on the redheaded owner's face was enigmatic and Whitney found it irritatingly unreadable. "I've got my ways," was all Miss Joan said.

"She's kidding, right?" Whitney asked in a hushed whisper.

Because she had turned her head away from Miss Joan and whispered her question to him, Liam felt Whitney's warm breath feathering along the side of his neck. It caused various internal parts of him to go temporarily haywire before he was able to summon a greater degree of control. When he finally did, it allowed him to shut down the momentary aberration and function normally again.

But for just a second, it had been touch and go.

"You'll know when Miss Joan is kidding," he promised Whitney.

"Let me show you to a table," Miss Joan offered. The words stopped short of being an order.

Miss Joan brought them over to a table on the side that was relatively out of the way of general foot traffic.

Once they were seated, the owner of the diner looked from Liam to his companion, as if to make a further assessment, and then asked, "So, what can I get for the hero and the rescuee?"

"I'm not a hero, Miss Joan."

"No point in denying what everybody's thinking,

boy," Miss Joan said. Then, looking at the young woman at the table, she confided, "He's always been a little on the shy side, downplaying things he's done." Her thin lips stretched out in a smile. "But you'll get to see that for yourself if you stay around here long enough."

"I'm sure I would," Whitney replied, thinking she might as well be polite and play along with what this woman was saying. "*If* I were staying, but I'm not. I'm just killing a little time here before I get back on the road."

Miss Joan smiled knowingly. "You go right ahead and do that, dear. You do that." Her tone of voice made it clear that she knew more about the situation than either the young woman or Liam. Amber eyes shifted to Liam. "Want your usual?"

Liam grinned and nodded. He viewed the meal as comfort food. He was about due for some comfort, he thought. "Yes, please."

"And you, honey?" Miss Joan asked, turning her gaze to Whitney.

"I'll have a cheeseburger and fries," she told the older woman.

"Coming right up," Miss Joan promised as she withdrew from the table.

Whitney noted that the woman hadn't written down either order. Lowering her voice, Whitney leaned in closer to the man who had brought her here in the first place.

"Is she always like that?" she asked once Miss Joan had withdrawn.

"Like what?" Liam asked, curious. As far as he was

concerned, it was business as usual for the owner of the diner.

"Invasive," Whitney finally said after spending a moment hunting for the right word to describe what she'd felt.

Liam turned the word over in his head, then shrugged. "I suppose so. That's just Miss Joan being Miss Joan," he said, then assured her, "I'll tell you one thing. There's nobody better to have on your side when you've got a problem or need a friend than Miss Joan."

Whitney glanced over her shoulder toward the older woman. The latter was behind the counter, engaging one of her customers in conversation as she refilled his coffee cup.

Aside from the fact that the woman seemed nosy, Whitney saw nothing overly remarkable about Miss Joan. The woman certainly didn't strike her as someone people would turn to in an emergency.

"Her? Really?" she asked Liam.

"Her. Really," he confirmed with a hint of an amused grin.

Whitney shook her head. "I'm afraid I just can't see it."

"Well, you're still an outsider so that's understandable. You'll have to experience it for yourself."

Whitney laughed shortly, waving the idea away.

"I'll pass on that, thanks. The second my car is back on solid ground, I'm out of here." She glanced at her watch and frowned. She was really behind schedule. "I should already be on my way."

"Maybe you should call whoever you're going to

see and let them know that you're being held up," Liam suggested.

Her eyes widened as she looked at him warily. "Held up?"

"Delayed," Liam amended.

"Oh."

Whitney chewed on her lower lip, thinking. She really didn't want to call to say she'd be late, but she had to grudgingly admit that the cowboy had a point. With that, she shrugged his jacket off, letting it rest against the back of her chair, and dug into her pocket for her phone.

Pulling it out, she began to tap out the phone number of the band she was on her way to audition. When nothing happened, she tried the number again—with the same result. Frustrated, she took a closer look at her phone and realized that it was completely dormant. The light hadn't really come on.

Why was it acting as if it was drained? "I just charged the battery," she complained.

Liam leaned over and placed his hand over hers, turning her phone so that he could get a better look at it. The diagnosis was quick and succinct.

"I think it's dead."

"Dead?" Whitney echoed. "How can it be dead?" she challenged.

He had an answer for that, as well. "That's not a waterproof case, is it?" He'd phrased it in the form of a question, but he already knew the answer.

"No," Whitney snapped. And then she remembered something. "But you dived in to pull me out of the water and you had your phone in your pocket," she recalled. "I saw you take it out to call that mechanic and whoever sent over that cherry picker."

Rather than say anything, Liam took out his phone and held it up to let her see the difference between his and the one she had in her hand.

"Mine's sealed in a waterproof case," he told her. She looked as if she was about to protest, so he explained rather matter-of-factly, "Things happen out here. All you can do is try to stay as prepared as possible."

Of course, he thought, he definitely wasn't prepared to be as strongly attracted to this woman as he was. But then, he'd never saved anyone from drowning before and maybe that had a lot to do with it.

Whitney was torn between actually *liking* the fact that he was this prepared and resenting the fact that he was taking charge like this while she couldn't. What was even worse was that she was having all sorts of feelings about this man that had absolutely nothing to do with any of this—except that he had saved her.

"Like a Boy Scout," she commented.

"Something like that, I guess. Want to borrow my phone to make that call?" he offered, holding it out to her.

"I guess I'm going to have to," she muttered, less than thrilled about this turn of events. She glared at her unresponsive phone. "I guess this is just an expensive paperweight now."

"Not necessarily," Miss Joan said.

Whitney nearly jumped out of her skin. The woman had seemingly materialized out of nowhere again. Didn't *anyone* else find that annoying? she couldn't help wondering.

Taking a breath to steady nerves that were becoming increasingly jumpier, Whitney turned in her seat and focused on what the older woman had just said rather than the fact that she was beginning to view Miss Joan as some sort of a resident witch.

"Do you think you can fix this?" she asked Miss Joan, allowing a trace of hope to enter her voice for good measure.

Miss Joan looked at the phone in question. "Depends. This just happened, right?" she asked, raising her eyes to look at Liam's companion.

"Right," Whitney answered quickly.

Miss Joan put out her hand. "Let me take your phone apart and put it in a container of rice."

"You're going to cook it?" Whitney asked warily.

Miss Joan laughed. "Hardly. Rice draws the moisture out. Doesn't work all the time but it's the only shot your phone has."

With a sigh, Whitney handed her phone over to the woman, although she was far from confident about what was about to transpire.

"Okay."

Taking the phone, Miss Joan pocketed it for a moment. "By the way, these are for you," she said, offering the younger woman what had caused her to return to the table before Angel had finished preparing their orders.

Whitney then noticed that the older woman had brought over a couple of items of clothing with her—a light blue sweatshirt and a pair of faded jeans.

Instead of taking the items, Whitney stared at them. "What am I supposed to do with these?"

Miss Joan pursed her lips, a sign that she was bank-

ing down a wave of impatience. "Well, this is just a
wild guess on my part, but if it were me, I'd put them
on. In case you didn't know, the clothes you have on
will dry a lot faster without you in them—especially
if I put them in a dryer. Unless, of course, you like
looking like something the cat dragged in," Miss Joan
added whimsically.

"Ladies' room is right through there," she told Whitney, pointing toward the far side of the diner. And then
she held the defunct phone aloft. "I'll go get your orders
after I put this baby into the rice container."

Whitney felt as if she'd just been doused by the flash
flood a second time, except that this time around, it
had come in human form.

After a beat, she gazed at Liam. "I think I'm beginning to see what you mean about Miss Joan."

"Miss Joan likes to look out for everybody," he explained. "Like a roving den mother. Takes some getting used to for some people. Now, I'm not telling you
what to do, but it might not be such a bad idea putting
those on." He nodded at the clothes she was holding
in her arms.

She'd felt rather uncomfortable in the wet clothes,
despite the jacket Liam had given her. But she hadn't
felt it was worth drawing attention to the fact. After
all, it wasn't as if anyone could do anything about it.
Except that obviously Miss Joan could—and had.

Whitney rose without saying a word and walked
to the rear of the diner, holding the clothes Miss Joan
had brought her.

She had definitely fallen down the rabbit's hole,
Whitney thought as she changed quickly, discarding

her wet outer garments and pulling on the sweatshirt and the jeans Miss Joan had given her.

Dressed, Whitney didn't know what surprised her more, that the strange woman with the flaming red hair had brought her a change of clothing—or that the clothes that Miss Joan had brought her actually fit.

"You look a lot drier," Liam commented with a smile when she finally returned and quietly slipped back into her chair.

Whitney's eyes met his. He couldn't quite read her expression. It seemed to be a cross between bewildered and uneasy.

"How did she know?" Whitney asked.

"That you were wet?" It was the first thing that came to his mind. "It might have to do with the fact that there was a small trail of water drops marking your path to the table."

He tactfully refrained from mentioning that both her hair and the clothes beneath his jacket were plastered against her body.

She shook her head. "No, I mean how did Miss Joan know what size I took? The jeans fit me as if they were mine." And she found that almost eerie.

Liam laughed again. These were things that he had come to accept as par for the course, but he could see how they might rattle someone who wasn't used to Miss Joan and her uncanny knack of hitting the nail right on the head time and again.

"Like I said before, that's all part of her being Miss Joan. The rest of us don't ask. We just accept it as a given."

The next minute, Miss Joan was at their table again.

This time Whitney didn't jump and her nerves didn't spike.

"You look better, honey," Miss Joan said with approval. She'd brought their orders over on a tray and now leaned the edge of it against their table. She proceeded to divvy the plates between them. And there was more.

"Figured you might like a hot cup of coffee with that." Although she had brought two coffees, she directed her comment to Liam. "It'll take the rest of the chill out of your bones," she promised with a wink that instantly took thirty years off her face.

The tray now emptied, Miss Joan deftly picked up the discarded blouse and tailored slacks from the floor next to Whitney's chair. "I'll just take care of these for you," the woman said.

"I usually have those dry-cleaned," Whitney protested as the other woman was beginning to walk away with her clothes.

Miss Joan paused, glancing down at the wet clothing she was holding. "I think we both agree that there's really nothing 'usual' about this now, is there?" she said knowingly.

With that, Miss Joan walked away.

Whitney glared at the man who was responsible for bringing her here in the first place. "Was she ever in the military?" she asked.

Liam laughed. It didn't take a genius to see where Whitney was going with this. He didn't want her wasting her time or her energy.

"I think it'll be a whole lot easier on you if you stop trying to figure Miss Joan out and just accept her as being a force of nature. That's what the rest of us have done. It's just simpler that way."

Whitney frowned to herself. If these people wanted to deceive themselves and think of the diner owner as some sort of a "chosen one," that was their prerogative. But brand-new clothes not withstanding, she wasn't about to have any of it. That was for people who couldn't think for themselves and reason things out.

Whitney suddenly turned toward him again and changed the subject entirely. "How long do you think it's going to take your friend to get my car down out of that tree?" she asked.

"Hard to tell since I've never known anyone to have gotten their car up a tree before," Liam freely admitted.

Maybe everything had finally gotten to her, or she was just getting giddy. Then again, perhaps it was the result of nearly drowning that did it, but Liam's answer, offered to her with a completely straight face, struck Whitney as being funny.

Not just mildly funny, but rip-roaringly, side-splittingly so.

She laughed at what Liam had said and once she started laughing, the jovial sound just seemed to feed on itself.

It was hard for her to stop.

Because her laughter was the infectious kind, Liam laughed right along with her. After a minute or so of this, he stopped abruptly to look at her closely. He wanted to ascertain that she wasn't tottering on the verge of hysteria. Laughter could so easily turn to tears.

But in this case, the laughter was a form of letting off tension and nothing more than that. Even so, Liam had to ask. "You all right?"

It took her a moment to answer because she had to get herself under control first. But when she did speak, she was truthful about it.

"I really don't know," she admitted. "I almost drowned in water that hadn't been there when I started out. For all I know, my car's still up a tree, my phone might very well be dead, I've got on someone else's clothes and I'm sitting in a diner run by a strange woman who acts as if she can read my mind, so I guess the answer's no, I'm *so* not all right."

Liam listened to her intently and only when she was finished did he venture to speak. He gave her some age-old advice.

"Maybe you should eat something. You might feel more up to dealing with all this on a stomach that's not empty," he suggested.

That almost drove her to another round of laughter. Whitney managed to hold herself in check at the last minute.

"You sound like my mother," she said, responding to his quaint advice. *Before she ran off,* she added silently.

"All things considered, I think I'd rather sound like your father," Liam countered, amused.

Whitney raised her eyes to his. Her father had been the one who had all but bred competition into her and her siblings. Her mother, on the other hand, had been the dreamer, the one whose temperament could withstand anything—or so she had thought until the day she wasn't there anymore.

The day her mother had left a note on the kitchen table to take her place.

"No, you wouldn't," she said. "Trust me," she added when Liam looked at her somewhat skeptically.

"I do," he told her simply. "I trust you, Whitney."

She had no idea why that affirmation warmed her the way it did, but there was no denying that she was definitely reacting to it in a positive way.

Whitney decided that Miss Joan had to have put something into her cheeseburger. That was the explanation she was going with since she had no room in her life for any more complications. And feeling any sort of an attraction for this cowboy was definitely a complication of the highest magnitude.

Chapter Five

Whitney glanced down at her watch for the umpteenth time. She tried not to be too obvious about it, but she had a feeling that she wasn't fooling the man sitting across from her.

With each minute that passed by, she was getting progressively antsy.

She had never been one to dawdle over her food—there was always too much to get accomplished for her to eat leisurely—but she had deliberately forced herself to eat slower this one time, hoping that once she was done with the meal, there would be some news about the state of her car.

But Liam's phone had not rung and she had just popped the last French fry into her mouth.

Now what?

Trying to contain her impatience, she said to Liam, "Maybe you should check your phone, just in case you shut off the ringer."

"I didn't," he told her. The diner was usually a noisy place and he hadn't wanted to take a chance on missing the mechanic's call. He knew how important it was to Whitney. "But even if I had, I'd feel the phone vibrating."

"Then maybe you accidentally shut your phone off altogether."

She knew she was reaching, but it would be night soon and she was supposed to have been at the audition she'd set up in Laredo first thing in the morning. Now all that careful planning was about to fall through, though she'd called to say she'd be late. At the same time, she didn't like falling so far behind in her schedule.

Whitney could just see her brother Wilson's smug face now, making no secret of the fact that he enjoyed watching her stumble and, even better, fall behind. Her position was technically lower than his within the company, but she still felt she was in competition with him. This sense of extreme competition was the way they had all been raised. Never once was the family unit stressed. For the Marlowes it was more of a case of every man—and woman—for themselves.

She did *not* want to wind up on the bottom of the heap—demoted to territory off the beaten path as far as finding talent was concerned.

"I definitely didn't do that," Liam assured her. To prove it, he dug out his phone and glanced at its screen before holding it up for Whitney to view. "See?"

She saw, all right. Saw that there was no message across the front of the screen announcing a missed call or a missed text communication.

"I see," she acknowledged quietly, frustration bubbling up in her voice.

"Don't worry," Liam told her. "Mick'll come through. He always has before. No reason to think he won't this time." And then he grinned his lopsided grin as the door to the diner opened and Mick walked in.

"Speak of the devil," Liam said with a laugh. "Mick, over here," he called out, raising his hand in the air to attract the mechanic's attention.

Standing just a little past the threshold, Mick was scanning the diner's occupants. When he saw Liam waving his hand, Mick's lips parted in what could be viewed as an attempted smile, the kind that made small children and smaller dogs uneasy because the expression looked more like a grimace than an actual smile.

Waving back, Mick quickly crossed to the table at the rear of the diner.

"I wasn't sure you'd still be here," the mechanic blurted out as he approached them.

Once at the table, instead of sitting down, he remained on his feet, as if he felt that he might have to dash off at any moment.

At any other time, Whitney might have attempted to indulge in a little small talk, just to be polite. But at this point, she felt as if her nerves had been stretched out to their full limit—plus 10 percent more. She desperately wanted to be on her way, so she made no comment on the mechanic's statement.

Instead, she got right down to business and asked, "How's my car?" Before he could respond, Whitney forced herself to ask another question, which she realized should have come first. "Did you get it down out of the tree?"

"Oh, yeah, we got it down," Mick told her with conviction.

She wasn't sure that she was comfortable about his tone of voice. "And the car's in one piece?" she pressed.

Her heart was speeding up a little as she braced herself—for what she wasn't altogether sure, only that whatever it would be, something told her that it wouldn't be good.

"Pretty much," Mick acknowledged. "One of the headlights is smashed, but that's no big deal."

Liam read between the lines. "What *is* a big deal?" he asked, well versed in "Mick-speak." The man was hiding something.

Mick began slowly, working up to what he assumed the woman would think was the bad part. "Well, the engine's flooded—I mean *really* flooded, so it's gonna take some time to dry out."

"What else?" Liam prodded.

Mick took a deep breath as if it physically hurt him to be the bearer of this news. "The alternator took a beating and it needs to be replaced."

"And you can do that, right?" Whitney asked somewhat apprehensively, watching his face as he answered. If he was lying, she hoped she could tell the difference.

"Oh, I can do that, sure," Mick said with enthusiasm. And then his voice fell as he added, "Once I get the parts in."

Whitney stared at the thin man. "You don't have an alternator?" she asked, having no idea what that actually was or what it did.

"I don't have *that* alternator," Mick explained. "I'm going to have to start calling around to a bunch of suppliers to see if I can find one and then get it sent here."

Whitney's stomach tied itself up in knots. "And how long is that going to take?"

Mick was nothing if not honest in his answer. "Well, I haven't started looking for it yet, so it's hard to tell."

"Then what are you doing here?" she asked, feeling the last of her nerves shredding. "Shouldn't you be calling around, trying to locate one?"

"Liam said to let him know when we got the car out of the tree, so I came here to tell him that we did," Mick informed her.

"Okay, fine, you told him. You told us," she amended. "I'll authorize you to do what you have to do to get my car running. I'll pick it up on my way back." She was aware of the fact that both men were now looking at her quizzically. Ignoring that, she pushed on. "Meanwhile, I'll rent one of your loaner cars."

"There's just one little thing wrong with that plan," Liam interjected.

Now, in addition to her stomach having tied itself up in one giant knot, it started to sink. This did not sound as if it would turn out well.

"And that is?" she asked, afraid to put what had just crossed her mind into words.

"Mick doesn't have any loaner cars," Liam said.

"You're not serious." She said the words so low, Liam wasn't sure if her voice was fading, or if this was the calm before the storm.

"I'm afraid I am," Liam replied.

Her eyes darted toward Mick, who had a sheepish expression on his face as he nodded.

"Does *anyone* in this town have a car I can rent?" Whitney asked in exasperation. When Liam shook his head, a growing sense of panic had her asking, "How about the car dealer?"

To which Liam said, "What car dealer?"

"You don't have a car dealer." It wasn't a question but a conclusion wreathed in mounting despair. "If there's no car dealership here, where do you people get your cars?"

Liam considered her question, then said, "That all depends on what direction we want to go in. There's a dealer in Pine Ridge—but he doesn't have cars to rent, either," he said, guessing where her question was ultimately going.

Whitney closed her eyes for a moment and sighed. "This is like a nightmare," she cried.

Liam had always been able to look on the bright side of things. It was a habit he'd picked up from Brett. His older brother never seemed to be defeated, no matter how bad things might get.

"It doesn't have to be," he told Whitney.

How could he even *say* that?

"Oh, no? Well, what would you call being trapped in a tiny town that isn't even on some of the maps of this region?"

His view of Forever was decidedly different than hers obviously was. "An opportunity to kick back for a few days and unwind," he suggested.

But Whitney heard only one thing. "A few *days*?" she echoed, horrified.

"Think of it as a vacation, honey," Miss Joan told her, not about to be left out. The woman scrutinized her for a moment. "Speaking of which, when was the last time you took one?"

Why did these people think they could just invade her life and ask personal questions like this? It wasn't any of their business. But her sense of survival trumped her feeling of outrage, so she answered the older woman. "I don't take vacations."

"Well, there you go," Miss Joan concluded with a

smart nod of her head. "This is the universe telling you that you need one."

"What I *need*," Whitney retorted through clenched teeth, her temper just barely contained, "is to have my car running."

"And you will," Mick assured her. "Just gotta get the parts."

"Parts?" Whitney echoed, stunned and dismayed. "A minute ago it was just one part, now it's 'parts'?" Just what was this con artist's game?

"Well, I thought I'd fix that headlight while I was waiting for the alternator," Mick replied honestly.

"Why stop there? Why not repaint the car while you're at it," Whitney said sarcastically, throwing up her hands in mounting frustration.

"You want me to?" Mick asked her in all innocent sincerity.

"I think you should just stick to getting that alternator and fixing the headlight—don't want some highway patrolman giving her a ticket now, do we?" Miss Joan said to the mechanic, keeping one eye on the young woman Liam had saved. "Go on, Mick," she urged. "Get started on her car."

"Can't really get started doing much tonight," he confessed.

"Then do what you can," Miss Joan encouraged.

"Right away, ma'am," the mechanic promised. He paused to tip his cap to Whitney, and then, the next moment, he was hurrying out the door.

It occurred to Whitney that this woman had no right to tell the mechanic to do *anything* that had to do with her car.

It also occurred to her that if she valued her sanity—

as well as other vital parts of herself—she should forego trying to argue the point with Miss Joan and just go along with what the woman said.

Besides, she had a larger concern at the moment. If she had to stick around this one-horse town, she was going to need somewhere to sleep.

She directed her question to Liam. "I don't suppose this place has a motel or, better yet, a hotel around somewhere?" She was hopeful, but at the center, she had an uneasy feeling she knew what the answer would be.

Which in turn meant that she was going to have to camp out—something that was completely unacceptable to her.

Beggars can't be choosers, Whitney.

"There's the hotel that's going up," Liam said, thinking out loud. "That's where the cherry picker came from," he reminded her.

"Going up," she echoed. "Doesn't exactly do me much good without walls."

Whitney was doing her best to remain as calm as possible despite the fact that part of her felt as if she was on the brink of a meltdown. For most of the past year, she had been going ninety miles an hour. To come to a skidding halt like this threw her completely off.

"Oh, it's got walls," Liam assured her, then amended, "At least the first floor does." He tried to remember what Finn had said about the progress being made. "I think there are a handful of completed rooms on the ground floor."

The rooms didn't do her any good if the hotel wasn't in business yet. "But it's in the middle of being built, right?"

"Right." Liam didn't see what the problem was for her. "So?"

For such a good-looking man, he was pitifully slow on the uptake, Whitney thought. She proceeded to spell it out for him.

"So that means that the hotel is not open for business yet."

"No," he agreed. "At least not to the general public." He took out his cell phone again and began to tap out a number on the keypad.

And what was that supposed to mean? She didn't see where he was going with this distinction.

"Well, I'm part of the general public," she pointed out. And that meant that it didn't matter how many finished rooms the hotel had, it was still in the process of being built. And that in turn meant that it was *not* open for business.

Holding up his hand to push back the unending flow of words that threatened to come out of this woman's mouth, Liam focused on getting the call he was making to go through. He needed to concentrate in order to word this just right once the person on the other end of the line picked up.

"You can bunk at my place for as long as you need."

The offer came out of the blue, pretty much in the same fashion that Miss Joan had a habit of turning up to take part in various conversations.

Whitney twisted around to look at the woman. "Excuse me?" she said uncertainly.

"I'm offering you a place to stay in case Liam's negotiations break down." Miss Joan nodded toward Liam, who was clearly talking to someone on the other end of the line.

Whitney frowned slightly. Had she actually heard the woman correctly?

"Wait, let me get this straight," she said to Miss Joan. "You'd actually take me in and let me spend the night in your place?"

"That's what I said," Miss Joan confirmed. "And the night after that if you need to." Miss Joan smiled tolerantly at the younger woman, the implication clear that at least for the moment, she viewed her to be slightly mentally challenged.

How could Miss Joan be so casual about inviting her to spend the night—or two—in her house?

"But you don't know me," Whitney pointed out.

Miss Joan looked entirely unfazed by what she was clearly suggesting. But the older woman played along, just for good measure.

"You got any Wanted posters out on you?" Miss Joan asked glibly.

"What? No, of course not," Whitney declared indignantly after she replayed the woman's words in her head.

Miss Joan lifted her shoulders and then let them drop indifferently. "Then that's all I need to know. For the record," she added, leaning in so that only Whitney could hear her clearly, "neither do I. So we should get along well enough. As long as you don't mind snoring. Henry makes enough noise to imitate two buzz saws, flying high."

"Henry?" Whitney echoed uncertainly.

"My husband." She had married the man over a year ago. As far as she was concerned, they were still on their honeymoon. "He's got a few quirks, but he's a good man at bottom."

"And he'd be okay with you taking in a stranger and having them stay over in your house?" Whitney asked in disbelief.

"Sure. Why wouldn't he?"

"Because I'm a *stranger*," Whitney repeated, stressing the word.

"A stranger's a friend whose name you haven't found out yet," Miss Joan informed her philosophically. "Offer's on the table, good for any time if Little Murphy can't get you a room at the 'hotel' that's going up," she said, crossing back to the counter.

Whitney could have sworn the woman was actually sauntering, moving her trim hips provocatively.

It took her a moment to realize that she was not Miss Joan's intended prime target audience. That honor belonged to several of the older men sitting at the counter itself. Cowboys, if she was going to judge them by their boots and hats.

She turned around just in time to see Liam terminate his call and put his cell phone away.

"I got you a room."

There was a layer of apprehension that was pressing down on her and it prevented Whitney from feeling relieved. "At the hotel?"

"At the hotel," he confirmed. It was obvious that he was rather pleased with himself.

"And it has walls?" she asked suspiciously. With these people, she felt that she needed to spell everything out and take nothing for granted.

He grinned. "It has walls."

She had learned a long time ago not to be trusting or to make what seemed like logical assumptions. A person could be easily misled that way. As for being trusting, well, that path just led to general disappointment. *That* was a lesson she'd learned from her mother— even though that hadn't been her mother's intention at the time.

"Four walls?" she asked.

"You can count them when we get there," Liam told her, not bothering to hide his amusement.

Getting up from the booth, he took out his wallet and extracted several bills.

She took her cue and felt around for her wallet. She'd put it into the borrowed jeans she had on when she switched clothes.

"How much is my share?"

Liam glanced at her. Making her pay her share hadn't even crossed his mind. That wasn't the way things were done around here.

"That's okay, I covered it."

"I pay my own way."

He watched her for a long moment, then said glibly, "Good to know. Let's go."

He was leaving the diner. She had no choice but to hurry after him—or be completely stranded.

"I don't want to be in your debt," she protested.

He stopped for a second to tell her, "There are two kinds of debt—the monetary kind and the emotional kind. While you try to figure out which kind bothers you more, I'll drive you over to the hotel," Liam informed her.

And with that, he placed his hand to the small of her back and proceeded to guide her out of the diner.

Watching them, Miss Joan smiled to herself. "Looks like another Murphy brother just might be about to bite the dust," she murmured to her customer as she refilled his empty coffee cup.

Joe Lone Wolf, the sheriff's chief deputy, glanced over his shoulder toward the door that was now closing. "Lot of that going around," he acknowledged quietly just before he took a sip of his coffee.

Chapter Six

Liam got out of his truck and made his way around to the passenger side. Whitney had made no move to get out of the vehicle. Instead, she was staring at the building he had parked in front of.

When he opened her door, there was suspicion in Whitney's eyes as she turned to him. "This isn't the hotel."

The building he had brought her to was a wide, squat two-story building with the name Murphy's spelled out in bright green lights.

"No," Liam agreed, "it's not the hotel."

This was a bar. Exactly what was this man up to? Her bravado went up several notches. "I thought you said you were taking me to the hotel."

"I am and I will," he assured her. "We just have to stop here first."

Whitney still wasn't budging. Granted the man had saved her life and been nothing but upstanding until this point—but maybe it was all leading up to something. She wasn't about to let her guard down.

"Why?" she asked.

"Because," he said patiently, "this is where the lady who's in charge of building the hotel is right now."

And he thought that since she was bending a few rules for him, the least he could do was show up and thank Connie in person.

"The hotel is being built by a woman?" Whitney asked in surprise. The frown on her face gave way to a hint of a smile. She had to admit what he'd just said intrigued her.

"Long story," Liam told her as he went on to give her the highlights. "Connie Carmichael was part of Carmichael Construction and she—"

"'Was'?" Whitney got out of the truck. The name sounded vaguely familiar. "What happened?"

The entrance to Murphy's was only a few feet away. "She decided to head up her own company and help renovate and restore sections of this town as well as on the reservation—"

Whitney stopped before the wide oak door. "You have a reservation?"

Liam paused. The woman was rapid firing her questions at him, not letting him catch his breath.

"You know, you might get the answers to your questions if you just give me enough time to talk," he pointed out, amused. Was this what it was like in the world she came from—everyone talking, nobody really listening?

When she continued looking at him expectantly, Liam had no choice but to continue. "Yes, we've got a reservation. Three of my best friends live there."

Liam pushed open the saloon's door. A blast of warm air, contrasting sharply with the winter breeze outside, hit them as they entered. A wall of noise accompanied it, enveloping them.

Being the only place in town to gather, other than

Miss Joan's diner, Murphy's always did a fair amount of business. The number of patrons varied. Tonight the place was packed to the point that maneuvering around presented a challenge.

Whitney looked around, trying to take in as much as she could. "Are you related to the Murphy who owns this?" she asked, raising her voice so Liam could hear her.

"I *am* the Murphy who owns this. Or at least one of them," he said. Since, for once, she hadn't interrupted him, he continued, all the while expertly guiding her to the bar. "The saloon used to belong to my dad, then my uncle Patrick when Dad died. We got it after Uncle Patrick passed away."

He had taken hold of her hand and was bringing her over to somewhere. Her curiosity made her follow without protest.

"'We'?"

He looked at her over his shoulder. "My two brothers and me."

They seemed to be doing a fair amount of business, she thought, looking around. The place looked like a gold mine waiting to explode.

"Who runs it?" she asked.

"We all do." Then, because he wasn't giving credit where it was due, Liam added, "But Brett calls the shots. He's the oldest and he's the one with the most business sense. C'mon, I'll introduce you."

She really didn't want to be introduced to anyone. All she wanted was to find a place to spend the night, then be on her way to Laredo in the morning—provided her car was running by then.

A peripheral movement caught her eye. The next

thing she knew, a tall, dark, handsome bartender was working his way over to them.

"Ah, the prodigal brother returns." Brett's easy gaze shifted to take in the woman standing beside his youngest brother. "And I take it that this is the damsel in distress that you rescued."

Liam nodded. "Whitney, this is my brother Brett, the one I was telling you about. Brett, this is Whitney Marlowe."

Brett extended his hand over the bar. "Pleased to meet you, Whitney. What'll you have? It's on the house."

She didn't want anything, but thought that might insult the man, so she said, "A ginger ale would be nice." She half expected to hear him scoff, but all he did was smile.

"Ginger ale coming up." Opening a small bottle, Brett poured the contents into a fluted glass and placed it in front of her.

"Does everything that happens to someone in this town get immediately broadcasted to the whole town?" Whitney asked.

"Pretty much," Brett answered without any hesitation or offense at her tone. "It's a small town. We look out for each other here."

"Speaking of looking," Liam interrupted. "Do you know where Finn and Connie are?"

"Probably with each other." A casual shrug accompanied the guess.

"I kind of figured that," Liam said wearily. "But where? I thought they'd be in here."

Brett paused to take Nathan McHale's glass and refill it. Nathan was their most faithful patron and even the most infrequent attendee knew exactly what the man's beverage of choice was without asking. A dark ale that was kept on tap. Nathan's mug remained filled until such time as one of them felt the man had had his quota for the night. Once in a while, that call was made too late and Nathan spent the hours between midnight and dawn as a guest of the city inside a jail cell.

"Why?" Brett asked his brother, covertly studying the woman Liam had brought in with him. "What do you need with Finn?"

"Actually, it's Connie I really want," Liam explained. "Finn got her to okay Whitney spending the night in the hotel."

"But it's not finished yet," Brett reminded Liam as he leaned forward and whispered that little detail to his brother.

"According to Finn, the ground floor's completed and that includes all the rooms on that level." Liam nodded toward the woman nursing her ginger ale. "Whitney needs a room for the night."

"What about the room over the saloon?" Brett suggested, raising his eyes upward to indicate the studio apartment all three of them had put to use one time or another. Shifting his attention to Whitney, Brett told her, "That's where Alisha stayed when she first came to Forever."

"Alisha?" Whitney looked to Liam for an answer.

"Brett's wife," Liam explained, then thought she might need a little more detail than that. "She came out here from New York to work at the clinic with our other doctor."

"Other doctor?" Whitney repeated. "Does that mean that this Alisha is a doctor, too?"

"That's what it means," Brett answered with a wide smile.

"He's had that silly grin on his face ever since he got Alisha to agree to be his wife," Liam said, shaking his head at his brother. "I guess love does that for some people."

"Just wait until it happens to you, little brother," Brett said.

"If it did, I sure wouldn't be walking around grinning like some loon," Liam kidded.

"We'll see," Brett replied.

Whitney felt as if she was being bombarded with too much irrelevant information and it was hindering her from processing the important information.

"What about that room?" she asked. Maybe it would be simpler if she just spent the night in the room above the bar. After all, she was already here.

The last time he'd seen the room, it had been in a state of disarray. The hotel rooms, according to Finn, were pristine. "Think of it as a last resort," Liam advised.

"Hey, I lived in that room for a while," Brett protested. That had been before Alisha had stayed there and before Finn had added on the bathroom for Alisha's usage.

"Which is why I'm labeling it as a last resort," Liam said. "You sure you don't know where Finn is?"

"Never said I didn't know. That was something you just assumed," Brett declared. "What I said was that he was with Connie."

"Okay, since you *didn't* say you didn't know, then can you tell me where he is?" The playful drawl had left Liam's voice, a sure sign that he was serious.

Rather than give him a verbal answer, Brett pointed over his brother's head. Turning, Liam scanned the immediate area and then spotted Finn. As predicted, the middle Murphy brother was with his fiancée.

Liam turned to glare at Brett. "Why didn't you say so to begin with?"

"And lose out on this fine, scintillating conversation we've been having?" Brett asked, feigning surprise.

Liam grunted dismissively at his brother. Instead of just walking away, he paused to take Whitney's hand, drawing her off the bar stool. He did it not because he found her to be a singularly stunning woman despite the fact that she had no makeup on, thanks to the flash flood, but because the saloon was filled to the brim with patrons. There was a distinct possibility that if he wasn't holding on to her, they might get separated and ultimately lose track of one another.

Granted the saloon wasn't big by most standards, but when it was packed the way it was tonight, getting lost in the crowd was all too easy a feat. Not only that, but he'd seen too many appreciative glances sent Whitney's way and he wanted to make sure that no one acted on impulse and cornered her.

"C'mon. Let's go," Liam said gently.

The second he had taken her hand, Whitney had felt it. Felt that strange magnetic pull, that intense crackle that instant chemistry generated.

Whitney did her best to block it without being obvious about it. She knew that if she pulled her hand out of his, she'd be drawing attention to herself for all the wrong reasons. And one look at her face in an unguarded moment would tell Liam far more than she was willing for him to know: that she was extremely attracted to him. Whether it was because he'd risked his life to save hers, she didn't know. What she did know was that what she felt was something that both of them would be far better off not having subjected to the light of day.

She had no time for complications—especially if that complication lived in such an out-of-the-way place as this one. Right now, her life was all about work. Later down the road, she'd concentrate on the personal aspects that were currently missing.

But not now.

The moment they came up to the people Liam was obviously seeking, Whitney immediately disengaged her hand from his. If he noticed the abrupt way she did it, he gave absolutely no indication.

"So you two need a room?" Finn asked innocently, looking from his brother to the woman standing next to him, a woman he didn't recall ever seeing before.

"*She* needs a room," Liam emphasized.

Finn flashed a smile at her, a smile she had already seen duplicated on both Brett's and Liam's faces. The family resemblance began with their smiles, Miss Joan was fond of saying.

"My brother has no manners," he told Whitney. Putting out his hand to her, he introduced himself. "Hi, I'm Finn. This is my fiancée—love saying that word," he confided. "Connie."

Whitney acknowledged both introductions, nodding her head as she shook hands with first one, then the other.

There was a vague resemblance between the brothers, she noticed. But Finn's hair was a light brown while

Liam's was a dirty blond that made her fingers itch to touch it.

With Connie, the second their eyes met, Whitney sensed a kindred spirit in the slender, auburn-haired woman. Maybe life here in this little dot on the map wasn't quite as laid-back as she thought.

"Pleased to meet you," Whitney murmured to both.

"What brings you to Forever?" Finn asked.

"The flash flood," Whitney replied without hesitation. If that hadn't occurred, she and her car would have been well on their way to Laredo.

"Then that story making the rounds is true?" Finn asked in surprise, looking from her to Liam for confirmation.

Liam's brother made it sound as if she was the town's breaking news story. Just how starved for news were the people in this town? she couldn't help wondering.

"Depends on the details in the story," Liam qualified cautiously. When he saw Finn begin to open his mouth to fill him in on just that, Liam cut him off. "But it's going to have to keep. I need to get Whitney to bed." When he saw his brother's face light up, he realized he hadn't exactly phrased that correctly. "To *a* bed. To her bed." Then, for good measure, he added, "She needs to get some rest."

At any other time, Liam would have gone out of his way to wipe that smug, amused look off his brother's face, but who knew where that would ultimately wind up. So for everybody's sake, he banked down his feelings.

"Here you go," Connie said, pushing a key card over to him on the table.

Liam was quick to lay his hand on the key card.

This, he assumed, was what they were using instead of a good old-fashioned key these days.

"Thanks, both of you," Liam emphasized, holding up the key card. He was looking directly at Connie as he said it.

"Don't mention it," Connie said. The smile on her lips was the kind someone had when they felt they were sharing some inner secret with the other party.

"A kindness should always be mentioned—and acknowledged," Whitney told the couple. Connie smiled at her.

"Ready to go?" Liam asked, just in case Whitney had changed her mind and wanted to stay for the music or the company, or for some other reason. He wanted to accommodate her, even though he wouldn't have been able to explain why. It was just something he felt.

Liam didn't have to ask her twice. Turning toward the front door, Whitney all but burrowed her way through the crowd in a matter of minutes.

"I guess that's a yes," he commented with a laugh, increasing his stride to keep up with her.

The lady could certainly hustle when she wanted to, he thought.

Having fallen a couple of steps behind her, Liam was afforded a rather enticing view of the way the jeans Miss Joan had given her adhered to her body, molding themselves to her hips with every step she took.

That alone was worth the price of admission—and any trouble he had to go through to accommodate the woman he had saved from a watery, albeit rather dirty, grave.

They got back into his truck and Liam drove her the short distance to the hotel.

"This is it?" Whitney asked as she got out on her side. She was staring at a building whose steel girders were up, but only the first floor bore any resemblance to an actual hotel.

"This is it," he confirmed. "Forever's very first hotel. C'mon, I'll take you inside," he coaxed.

"Give me a minute," she requested. "I'm trying to decide if I've just made a mistake."

"To spend the night here?" he guessed. "Don't worry. It gets better once you're inside."

"It would have to," she said under her breath.

Judging by what she saw, the first floor did look to be finished. But when she raised her eyes to take in the other floors—floors that were in various degrees of completion—that was when she realized just how much more work there was left before this could officially become an actual hotel.

She started to walk toward the unfinished building, emulating a moth drawn to a flame.

"Wait a second," Liam told her as he went rummaging through an area in the rear of the truck. It took him a minute, but he found what he was looking for and held it aloft.

It was a lantern.

An uneasy feeling zipped through her as she looked at what he was holding. "What's that for?" she asked.

"I doubt if the power's been turned on yet," he told her honestly. "This'll give you light for the next fourteen hours."

She had no intentions of being here that long. "That's okay, I don't need it," she told him.

"Yes, you do," Liam insisted, taking the lead and

walking ahead of her. "Unless you glow in the dark, you're going to need to see where you're going."

It was twilight and she was exhausted, but nonetheless, she stubbornly held her ground. "It's a hotel. It'll have an emergency generator."

"Only if it had electricity turned on in the first place— and it hasn't. It's an *unfinished* hotel," he stressed. "Plenty of places for you to have an accident. So take it." He all but slapped the lantern into her hand. He wanted her to get used to carrying it.

She blew out a breath, grudgingly—and silently— admitting he was right. But out loud she said, "Anyone ever tell you that you are pushy?"

"Nope. They're all too busy thanking me for keeping them from doing something stupid," he informed her as they entered the hotel through the front entrance. He took in his surroundings, recalling the recent tour he'd been given by Finn. Even so, it took him a moment to get his bearings.

"It's through here." He indicated a corridor on his left.

Because Whitney had no idea which way she was supposed to go, she let him lead the way.

Since none of the rooms were occupied, Liam chose what he assumed was the largest room—a corner suite—for her.

"How about this one?" he asked, stepping inside the suite.

She peered over his shoulder, then stepped inside, still looking around. Whitney made her way over to the sliding glass door that led to a small balcony. "It'll do," she said.

He noticed a lack of enthusiasm in her voice. "What's wrong?" he asked.

Ordinarily, she would have told him he was imagining things. But she was tired and overwrought, so the truth came out despite the fact that she found her admission to be somewhat embarrassing.

"I don't think I'm going to be able to sleep tonight."

He made a guess as to the cause. "Worried about the meeting you're missing?"

She shook her head. That was small potatoes, actually. "It's not even that. It's dark around here and it's really quiet." He was obviously waiting for more. Her smile was rueful. "I can't sleep without noise and some sort of light peeking in through my bedroom window." She ran her hands up and down her arms, trying to ward off the chill she felt. "Quiet like this just feels eerie to me."

He'd always loved the quiet, but he supposed there were obviously those, like Whitney, who didn't. "Where did you say you were from?"

"Los Angeles."

He laughed shortly. He'd never been but he knew what she was getting at. "That explains it. Well, give it your best shot," he encouraged. "See you in the morning."

Whitney nodded, resigning herself to sleeping in snatches. She could feel the disquietude settling in. "Thanks for everything."

"Don't mention it," he said as he walked out.

But rather than going back to Murphy's or turning in for the night himself—God knew he deserved some sleep himself—Liam got into his truck and began to drive slowly back and forth around the corner of the hotel, exactly where her room was located. He put his headlights on bright and turned up his radio, creating both noise and light.

Inside, Whitney had lain down, fully clothed, on the bed, hoping to hypnotize herself into falling asleep. Her concentration was interrupted by a sudden burst of light and a throbbing noise that passed for current music. The fact that there were both out here mystified her.

She got off the bed, opened the sliding glass door and stepped out onto the terrace.

That was when she saw him. Saw the lone truck driving around in what amounted to elongated circles near her hotel suite.

Liam.

Watching him for a moment before she withdrew into her room again, Whitney found herself smiling.

This was, she thought, the nicest thing anyone had done for her in a very, very long time.

Chapter Seven

"You're *what*?"

Whitney held her newly restored cell phone—thanks to Miss Joan's container of rice—away from her ear as her brother Wilson's loud rant came through loud and clear.

No signal failure here, she thought as she continued to hold the phone she'd found outside of her door this morning away from her ear.

After a second, feeling that it was safe, she brought the cell phone closer to her ear again.

"I said," she repeated patiently, "I'm going to be stuck here for a few days."

She hadn't expected sympathy from Wilson and that was just what she got—none. "You mean you're slacking off," he accused angrily.

"No, I mean exactly what I said," she told him as calmly as she could—she'd learned a long time ago that shouting at Wilson never got her anywhere. "I'm stuck here. My car needs to have several parts replaced before it's drivable again."

"So what's the problem?" he asked, his voice going up another octave.

"The parts have to be ordered."

Mick had already called her earlier this morning to say that he'd made the necessary calls to get her vehicle up and running and her back on the road—but it was going to take at least a couple of days. She'd thanked him for the update, and then immediately resigned herself to breaking the news to her brother in LA.

"A couple of days? Where the hell are you, the Amazon rain forest?" he retorted.

"No, actually quite the opposite. It's pretty dry here—except yesterday when it flooded."

Whitney had to admit that she was still mystified how a few minutes of intense rain could have suddenly immersed her in a small lake. Mystified as well as rather shaken up because she was just now coming to terms with how close she had come to losing her life. She was certain that she would have, had it not been for Liam.

"I already gave you all the details," she told Wilson.

It was obvious by his tone that he'd thought she was just exaggerating. "Yeah, yeah. All I hear is that you're slacking off."

"Slacking off?" she echoed, her voice finally rising. Wilson was pushing her to the edge of her patience. "I almost died yesterday," she reminded him angrily.

"Uh-huh. And if you don't sign up that band, and several more really good ones, our label might be in danger of going belly-up, remember?" he said. "We're only as good as the new artists we sign up."

Wilson had a tendency to exaggerate and dramatize everything. Ordinarily, it didn't faze her and she just shrugged it off. But today it irritated the hell out of her.

So much so that she heard herself saying, "Look, if

you're so worried about missing out on that band, why don't you send Amelia to sign them?"

"Amelia," he repeated as if their cousin's name was brand-new to him.

"Amelia," Whitney said with more conviction.

"You're serious."

She and Amelia had been competitors since pre-school. The fact that they were first cousins had no bearing in their rivalry. From time to time, there was a marginal effort to get along, but what they really enjoyed was outdoing the other. Getting The Lonely Wolves to sign with Purely Platinum, the family label, would have been a decent feather in either one of their caps.

Whitney sighed. She hated giving up this opportunity, but the recording label was more important than any one person, and that included her.

"You need the band, or more to the point, you need a band or an artist to put you back on the map and I can't very well hitchhike all the way to Laredo. So yes, I'm serious."

"Okay, just remember, you passed up on this," Wilson told her.

"I'll get the next one," Whitney responded, trying her best to sound upbeat.

She heard Wilson grunt dismissively. "*If* there's a next one for you. You know this business, Whit. You're only as good as your next success. Barring that, you're history."

She'd expected just a hint of support from her brother. After all, she had been there for him. Granted they were all competitive in her family, but when had it become cutthroat?

"Wilson, after all the time I've put into the company—" But she found herself talking to dead air. Her brother had hung up on her.

Frustrated, Whitney vented the only way she knew how. She let loose with a guttural cry that was a cross between anguish and anger. After having emitted the teeth-jarring sound, she hurled her cell phone across the room. It hit the door with a loud thud and then fell to the floor, miraculously still intact.

Padding across the carpeted floor in her bare feet, Whitney stooped down to pick up her phone. She was still crouching when she heard a sharp knock on the door less than half a minute after her momentary tantrum.

She thought of ignoring whoever was on the other side of the door, but since she was the only person who had a suite—or a room of any kind—in the hotel, she felt obligated to respond. It might be the contractor coming to tell her that she couldn't stay here any longer.

Holding her breath, she approached the door and asked, "Who is it?"

"Liam Murphy. You okay in there?" he asked. "I heard a scream and then something falling and I just want to make sure you're all right."

Whitney lost no time in flipping open the lock and opening the door to the suite. "Not really," she said, answering his question.

She was far from a happy camper at this point. She'd just lost out signing what might become a major new band, moreover she had lost out to Amelia, who would rub her nose in it for weeks to come—maybe even months. If she lasted that long.

"Anything I can do?" he asked her, walking into the suite.

He actually sounded genuine in his offer. She had already decided, after last night's above-and-beyond performance, that Liam Murphy was not only exceptionally handsome, he was exceptionally kind and selfless, as well. If she was in the market for someone to share her life with—which she wasn't—he would have made an excellent choice.

But this was not the time to entertain any romantic thoughts. She needed instead to assess Liam's appeal dispassionately. With his somewhat longer dirty blond hair and electric blue eyes, not to mention that easy, sensual smile, Liam would undoubtedly be the center of every female's dreams from fourteen to ninety-four. She definitely wouldn't do well against competition like that.

As it was, she laughed softly at his offer. "How are you at laying your hands on a car and healing it?"

"That, unfortunately, is entirely out of my league."

"That's what I was afraid of. Then no, there's nothing you can do for me." She walked back toward the sliding glass door and looked out. In the distance, she could make out a range of foothills. "I need to be in Laredo today and it's just not going to happen."

He came up behind her, his attention focused on her. He really wanted to help. "What's in Laredo?"

· "A band. The Lonely Wolves," she told him. What was the point of even talking about it, she thought, dejected. Amelia was going to sign them up and she'd suddenly be transformed into the lead weight that was being carried by the label. Temporarily.

"You don't look like a groupie," he commented.

The term caught her by surprise and she laughed shortly. "Good, because I'm not."

Something wasn't adding up. "Then why all this angst about a four-piece band?"

He'd surprised her again. She had him pegged as a fan of country music, not hard rock. "You've heard of them?"

"Sure I've heard of them," he acknowledged.

He was keenly aware of most of the homegrown bands in the southern part of Texas. He didn't see any of them as competition but as opportunities for a learning experience. His musical education came from all over and he soaked it up like a sponge.

"They were the people I was going to be meeting with today. Actually, I wasn't 'meeting' with them so much as auditioning them, but even that was just a technicality. Unless they didn't perform as well in person as they did on the demo they had sent in, I was going to be signing them for the label I represent."

He stared at her, wondering if he was still asleep and dreaming. This was just too much of a coincidence to actually be true. What were the odds that he would wind up rescuing someone who worked for a music label?

"You're a talent scout?" he asked, doing his best to sound casual about it. Since he and his band were unknowns, he couldn't push too hard—but he did want her to hear them.

She nodded. "My grandfather founded Purely Platinum Records and my brothers, cousins and I all work for the label. My older brother, Wilson, runs the company these days after my father passed away at his desk two years ago."

"I'm sorry," Liam said with genuine feeling.

She shrugged. "It happens." She hadn't been close to her father. He tended to favor her brothers, but in her heart of hearts, she still missed him. "We usually have at least a handful of big names signed at any one time," she confided, "but times have been tough lately. Our star performers were lured away to other labels and Wilson's trying to get fresh blood to bring us back to the top."

She looked as if she had just lost her best friend and it prompted him to ask, "If you're trying to get the label back on its feet, why do you look so down?"

"Because," she said between clenched teeth, "I just had to tell Wilson to send my cousin Amelia to sign the group."

Liam still didn't see the problem. "And…?"

Whitney knew that this had to sound petty to Liam, but she wasn't about to sugarcoat it. "And she's been out to top me since before we took our first steps."

"And I take it that whoever signs this band up first goes to the head of the line?"

She shrugged again. It was pointless to talk about this. Whatever happened, happened. "Something like that," she murmured.

It took him less than a minute to make up his mind. It wasn't his day to man the bar, so he was free to make this offer. "I can drive you to Laredo."

Struggling not to give in to feeling sorry for herself, she had barely heard what Liam had said. And what she *thought* he'd said was impossible. "Excuse me?"

"I said I can drive—"

She waved away the rest of his words as they replayed themselves in her head. "I heard, I heard," she cried happily. "You'd do that?" she asked in disbelief.

"Yes."

"Why?" She had to know. "Why would you go out of your way like this for someone you don't even know?"

"Because it seems so important to you. And I did have a hand in saving your life, so that gives us a kind of bond," he said. "I want you to be happy living the life I saved."

The man was practically a saint, she thought. Excited, relieved and feeling suddenly almost euphoric, Whitney threw her arms around his neck and declared, "You're a lifesaver." She said it a second before she kissed him.

She only meant for it to be a quick pass of her lips against his, the kind of kiss one good friend gives another, because he certainly qualified for that distinction.

But at the last second, Liam had turned his head just a fraction closer in her direction and somehow what began as a fleeting kiss turned into something that was a great deal more.

Something of substance and depth.

Something to actually sing about.

Whitney felt herself responding instantly and before she could hold back—she didn't. Instead, almost moving on automatic pilot, his arms went around her, closing in an embrace that pressed her body against his.

That, too, brought a reaction with it, because every fiber of her being went on high alert.

This, the thought telegraphed through her brain, *is different.* Everything in her life before this moment was just a stick-figure drawing, executed in crayon, and this, what she was experiencing now, was a rich oil painting that instantly captured the viewers and drew them in.

It certainly did her.

The kiss went on far longer than either one of them had intended, taking on a life of its own and changing *their* lives from that moment on.

The exuberance she had initially felt, the exuberance that had generated this kiss in the first place, flowered and intensified, stealing her very breath away in the process.

Whitney's whole body suddenly ignited and had Liam's arms not gone around her when they did, she seriously felt that she would *not* be standing up right now. A wave of weakness had snaked through her, robbing her of the ability to stand. Forcing her to cling to him in order to remain upright.

And be thrilled about doing it.

For most of her thirty years, Whitney had been focused on getting ahead, on besting her siblings and cousins, because that was the way she—and they, even her cousins—had been raised by her father. And that sort of sense of intense competition did not allow anything else to interfere, did not allow anything else to flourish, even briefly.

She'd had a handful of dates so far, none of which were inspiring enough to turn her attention away from the family business and all the alert competitiveness it required.

She'd certainly never encountered anything remotely like this—or even dreamed of its existence.

But the longer the kiss continued, the less control

Whitney realized that she had over her own thoughts, her own body.

It was as if the very life force within her was being systematically sucked *out* of her.

She couldn't be doing this.

She *shouldn't* be doing this.

With her last ounce of self-preservation, Whitney put the heels of her hands against Liam's rock-hard shoulders and pushed him back.

The force she exerted didn't have the intensity required to crush a newborn ant, but it did get its point across to Liam.

Mainly because he felt he shouldn't have allowed it to go this far, at least, not this quickly.

Not yet.

Still, he couldn't do anything about the wide smile on his face. There was absolutely no way he could wipe it away or camouflage it as he stood looking at her after the fact.

The kiss made him feel like singing—as did Whitney.

"If I had known it meant so much to you and that you'd react this way, I would have offered to drive you there five minutes after I rescued you yesterday," he told Whitney.

Shaken by what she'd felt, she did her best to seem nonchalant. Despite her performance, she had a feeling that she hadn't convinced Liam that his kiss had no effect on her.

Still, he seemed nice enough to pretend to go along with her charade.

"Well, there's no time like the present. Just let me make a couple of calls to update everyone," she said, crossing back to the table, where she had left her cell phone.

God, did her voice sound as squeaky to him as it did to her?

Clearing her throat, Whitney picked up her phone and prepared to make her first call. She raised her eyes to his and waited.

Liam took the hint. "I'll just go to Miss Joan's and get us a couple of breakfasts to go," he offered.

She nodded, barely hearing him. Had she heard, she would have again been struck by his thoughtfulness. But right now, she was struggling to regain some control over herself.

The first number she dialed was her brother's.

Wilson answered on the third ring.

"Wilson, it's Whitney."

"Now what's wrong?" he demanded wearily.

Sometimes she really disliked his negative approach to everything.

"Nothing. Just tell our illustrious cousin Amelia to put her broom back in the closet. She won't be flying to Texas to sign that Laredo-based band."

She could hear her brother come to life. It was there in the very way he breathed. She could tell he was all ears now.

"What happened?" he asked.

"Nothing happened," she said, deciding to play this out a little. "I just found a way to get to Laredo and since I'm already in Texas, there's no point in her coming out, too. It's as simple as that."

"She already said yes," Wilson told her, as if no changes to the plan were acceptable.

What had it been? Five minutes since she'd spoken to him? Talk about acting quickly...

"Well, now *you* can say no. I'll call you once the band has signed the contracts—*if* they're as good as that demo they sent," she said, and then it was her turn to terminate the call without forewarning.

It was also before her brother could offer any more protests.

Her second call was to the band itself, to tell them that the canceled audition was back on again, only she needed to schedule it for a slightly later hour than had initially been agreed to.

"So you can audition for me at around three," she informed them cheerfully.

"No, I'm afraid that we can't," the lead singer replied.

It was time to go into saleswoman mode, she thought. It wouldn't be the first time. She'd started out as a somewhat precocious child and what she had going for her then was her innocent face. Now she had her looks and her innocent manner, both of which she used with expert precision.

"Look, if you're thinking of signing with someone else, I just want you to know that we have the better reputation because we've been in the business for over fifty years—not to mention that we have far better perks for our top draws."

"Yeah, yeah, I know all that," the man on the other end of the line said, cutting her short. "But right now, we can't audition for you because we don't have a drummer."

Caught off guard, Whitney's mouth dropped open.

Chapter Eight

Maybe she'd heard him wrong, Whitney thought. "What do you mean, you don't have a drummer?" she asked the man on the other end of the call.

"I don't have a drummer," Kirk, the lead singer of The Lonely Wolves, repeated. "The guy's in the hospital."

This couldn't be good. "What happened?" she asked.

Part of Whitney was instantly sympathetic, but part of her couldn't help wondering if this was some sort of ploy, either in a bid to make their signing price higher, or to keep her label at bay while they auditioned for another talent scout, trying to see who would come through with the better offer.

"We were rehearsing, getting ready for the audition, and suddenly Scottie—the drummer—grabbed his stomach and doubled up. We all thought he was just clowning around and told him to get serious, but then he fell on the floor, still holding on to his stomach, except that now he was saying things like he feels his gut's on fire and he's dying, stuff like that. So we got him into my van and I drove like crazy over to the closest ER."

Kirk paused dramatically, catching his breath, then

continued, talking even faster than he had been a second ago. "They wound up operating on him right there in the ER. Turned out Scottie's appendix blew up or something like that."

"Is he all right?" Whitney asked, concerned.

"Yeah. Takes more than a crummy appendix to take Scottie out. But he feels awful now," Kirk added in a hushed voice.

Whitney laughed shortly. By her calculation, the drummer had just been operated on less than twenty-four hours ago. "I don't wonder. He went through a lot."

There was silence on the other end, as if Kirk was assimilating what she'd just said before responding. "What? No, I mean because he can't play, which means he blew the audition for the band."

The band's temporary derailment gave her some needed breathing space, Whitney thought. Funny how things can sometimes turn out for the best in the long run.

"Tell your drummer not to worry. We'll just reschedule the audition when he's up to playing," she told the lead singer.

More silence, as if she'd just managed to stun Kirk. "You mean it?"

Whitney smiled to herself. "Absolutely. Just tell Scottie to get better and I'll check in on you in a month."

"Are you just being nice?" Kirk asked, obviously leery of hoping for a second chance.

Whitney knew exactly where the performer was coming from. The world of entertainment was a fickle, completely unpredictable place. People who were at the top one month were thrown off and trampled by the

up-and-comers the following month. Staying power
was an art form as well as unusually rare.

"Yes, I mean it—but I'm also nice," Whitney said
as she smiled to herself.

She proceeded to take down an alternate number
where the lead singer could be reached and subsequently gave him her cell number, as well. Only then
did the singer decide that she was on the level.

The moment she terminated her call to the drum-
merless band, Whitney placed another call, this one
to her brother.

Again.

It was his private line, but even so, Wilson took his
time picking up. Whitney was getting ready to leave
a message on his voice mail when her brother finally
got on the line.

In place of a greeting, Wilson said, "Maybe we
should just string up two tin cans and use those every
five minutes." Impatience fairly throbbed in his voice
as he said, "What now, Whitney?"

"'Now' is when I tell you that not only don't you
have to send Amelia to audition The Lonely Wolves—
and, yes, I know you, Wilson, you were going to let
her fly down and show up even though I told you I was
going—but now I'm not going, either."

She heard her older brother sigh deeply. "What is
this, Whitney, reverse psychology so I decide *not* to
send Amelia in your place?"

"No, this is I'm not going because the band is down
one drummer. And let's face it, he's the best one in the
group *and* he's the one who writes the songs. You can
go right ahead and send Amelia if you want, but she
won't have anyone to audition once she gets there."

"What the hell happened to the drummer?" Wilson demanded angrily. "Is he hungover?" he guessed. "Or is it worse?"

Whitney pretended to think it over for a minute, just to keep her brother dangling.

"That all depends on whether or not you consider appendicitis to be worse than a hangover," she replied in a serious voice.

"He has appendicitis?" Wilson sounded rather unconvinced.

"Had," Whitney corrected. "Right in the middle of band rehearsal the way I hear it. Kirk—"

"And who the hell is Kirk?" Wilson asked.

"The lead singer," she said, sounding as calm as he was agitated. "Will, you *have* to make an effort to learn their names if you're signing them."

"Yeah, yeah," he said dismissively. "Get on with the story."

"Kirk rushed him to the hospital and the upshot, barring some bizarre disaster, is that the drummer is going to be fine. Just not up to playing right now. The band is rather bummed out about not auditioning for Platinum so I don't think we have to worry about them holding out to sign with another label," she told her brother.

"Is your car still in need of parts?" Wilson asked.

"Yes. What's one thing got to do with the other?" she asked.

And then it hit her. The answer to her question was right there in front of her. She just had some trouble getting herself to believe it since she had always been so honest and up-front about everything.

"You thought I made it up, didn't you?" she accused Wilson.

"Yeah, well, I thought you were just trying to get a little downtime for a change. By my reckoning, you've been going nonstop for practically years now—"

"No 'practically' about it, Will," she said, interrupting. "It *has* been years. I'm just as invested in our recording label as you are. If I'd wanted time off, I would have said so."

There was only one way to deal with Wilson and that was head-on. She'd learned that during her first negotiation for him. Older sibling or not, the man took absolutely no prisoners.

"Okay. Sorry." Wilson uttered the word rather grudgingly.

She knew he really wasn't sorry, but paying lip service was better than nothing, she supposed. So he said the word and she pretended to accept it.

"I'll give you a call as soon as I can get out of this one-horse town," she promised.

"Right."

And then, as usual, Whitney found herself listening to the sound of silence. Wilson had hung up.

"Someday, Wilson, someone is going to have to teach you some phone etiquette. And while they're at it, some regular etiquette wouldn't be out of order, either." She addressed the words to her dormant cell phone, which was now lying on the bed.

"Is that a new feature on your cell phone?" Liam asked, peering into the suite. "You talk to it and somehow messages magically get delivered?"

Beckoning for him to come in, she smiled a little

ruefully. "I'm just clearing the air by yelling at my brother."

Liam laughed shortly. "I kind of got that part." He'd heard her voice before he opened the door. "Anything wrong?" he asked seriously.

"Nothing a long stint in rehab wouldn't fix," she quipped.

Liam looked surprised. She'd made it sound as if her brother was in a position of considerable responsibility. "He's got a substance abuse problem?"

"No, my brother's got a people abuse problem," she corrected with a resigned sigh.

Liam had a simple question for her. "Why do you take it?"

There were lots of reasons, she thought. "Because I like my job. Because it's the family company. And because I've never known anything else. I think I was born traveling and auditioning performers, looking for just the right ones for our label."

He could see how hard it would be to give up something she cared about. But if her working conditions were unacceptable, then she needed to think over other paths she could take.

"You can always reeducate yourself, go off in a different direction," he suggested.

"Not hardly," she muttered. If she was going to spend that much energy, she would put it toward straightening things out on the home front. "Funny advice coming from a guy who works at the family business."

He supposed they had that in common, but the similarities ended there. Brett treated him with respect. That wasn't to say that his older brother didn't enjoy putting the screws to him once in a while. But the bottom line was Brett and Finn had his back and he had theirs.

"Just part-time," Liam told her.

He didn't want to talk about his actual passion—at least not until the timing was right. He was worried that she would get the wrong idea, that he'd been playing her all along, trying to cash in on the fact that he had saved her life and then trade that for a recording contract with her label.

He didn't want anything he didn't honestly earn.

"I've got breakfast," he said, holding up a bag. "You ready to hit the road?"

How quickly things can change, she couldn't help thinking. "Actually, turns out that there's no need for any road-hitting—not that I don't appreciate your volunteering and coming to my rescue this way. *Again,*" she emphasized.

"Nobody's keeping count," he said dismissively, then asked a more serious question. "Did your brother fire you?"

The question took her by surprise, as did his tone of voice. She could have sworn there was an underlying, albeit suppressed, indignation in his voice, strictly on her behalf.

"No—and he really *can't* fire me from the family company." Although, she thought, if he wanted to, Wilson could have made life a living hell for her. And *that* would convince her to leave.

"Anyway, it seems that the band's drummer had appendicitis and was brought to the hospital just in the nick of time. Everything went well, but he won't be holding a pair of drumsticks for a few weeks, so the audition's been postponed."

He wondered if that meant she'd stick around, or if that was a signal for her to leave. He knew the car would have to be left behind, but there were ways to ship out a vehicle to its final destination. He was hoping she'd go along with the first choice.

"So what now?"

Whitney shrugged. She hadn't thought that far yet. "I have breakfast, twiddle my thumbs. Wait for Rick to get my car running—"

"Mick," Liam corrected.

She flushed. "Right. Mick. Sorry," she murmured. "I really appreciated your volunteering to drive me down to Laredo, but since the trip is now off, you don't have to feel like you need to hang around." Although, she added silently, she really hoped that he would. "I've taken up too much of your time already."

"Well, seeing as I've got nothing planned since I'm not driving to Laredo, why don't we have breakfast together and then see where the day goes?" he suggested. After the way she had all but knocked his socks off earlier, he wasn't eager to part company just yet. "You want to eat here, or would you rather we go back to the diner and have our breakfast there?"

"You mean eat takeout in?" she asked, not entirely clear on what he was proposing they do. "Won't Miss Joan think that's kind of strange?"

Liam laughed. "Miss Joan's been subjected to a lot stranger things than that."

Well, if he didn't mind, why should she? And after what had transpired between them earlier, she thought it might be safer for both of them if they had people around instead of staying by themselves. She still didn't know what to make of the effect he'd had on her.

"All right, then, let's eat there," she agreed.

"You're on," he said, grinning.

"SOMETHING WRONG WITH the order?" Miss Joan asked when she saw the two of them walk into the diner fifteen minutes after Liam had picked up two breakfasts to go. "You two should have been on your way to Laredo by now," she estimated.

Whitney saw no point in asking the other woman how she knew about Laredo. Whitney was beginning to accept the fact that if there was anything to know about anyone, Miss Joan had homed in on it and already knew. She supposed that feeling this way gave her something in common with the rest of the citizens of Forever.

Instead of answering the older woman's question, Liam looked to Whitney as if silently asking if she minded his telling Miss Joan why they were there.

Rather than nod, Whitney did the honors herself. "The trip's been postponed, Miss Joan. Liam thought it would be more comfortable eating in here than in the hotel suite. I agreed, so here we are," she explained simply.

Miss Joan nodded her approval. "Makes sense. Find a table, I'll bring coffee."

"We've already got coffee," Liam told her, indicating the two containers he took out of the large bag. He placed the containers on the table.

Miss Joan waved her hand at the containers. "That coffee's at least forty minutes old. I'll pour you both fresh cups," she said in a voice that was not about to take no for an answer.

"She certainly does take charge, doesn't she?" Whitney whispered to him as she leaned across the small table Liam had picked.

"She likes to mother people," Liam explained.

Whitney wasn't entirely convinced. "That's one way to describe it."

"Hey, since you're gonna be with us for a bit," Miss Joan said to Whitney, filling the cup in front of her to an inch below the rim, leaving room for the cream, "how would you feel about coming out with us and helping pick out a Christmas tree?"

"Us?" Whitney repeated, a little confused as to what the diner owner was proposing.

"The town," Miss Joan clarified. "Each year, a bunch of Forever's citizens go out, scout the area, look for the best specimen to cut down and bring back," Miss Joan went on to explain.

"The tree's for the town square," Liam told her, filling in some of the gaps that Miss Joan had left. "After we bring it back and get it up, everybody gets a chance to decorate the tree."

It sounded like a really lovely tradition, Whitney thought. But it wasn't her tradition and she felt as if she would be intruding if she joined in.

"But isn't that a community thing?" Whitney pointed out as tactfully as she could.

"Yes…" Liam stretched out the word, waiting to see where Whitney was going with this.

"But I'm not part of the community." She doubted that everyone would be all right with her intrusion— and she couldn't fault them for it.

"Well, if you don't want to—" Miss Joan began, one rather bony shoulder rising and falling in a careless shrug.

"I didn't say that," Whitney protested.

The words had tumbled out of her mouth rather quickly before she had time to think them through. But even as she said them, Whitney figured that joining in might be fun. It had been years and years since she had gotten involved in something just for the sheer enjoyment of it. Everything had always had to have a purpose, an endgame attached to it.

But she was definitely willing to try a little fun.

"Good," Miss Joan said with finality. "Now eat up," she ordered. "The scouting trucks leave in half an hour."

Whitney could feel Liam staring at her in what could only be termed amazement as Miss Joan withdrew to make certain that this year's team was almost ready to set out on their quest.

Whitney could only shake her head in wonder. Miss Joan would have made one hell of a dictator, she thought. "You heard the lady, Liam," she said, turning toward him. "Eat up."

The sound of Liam's laugh as he dug in to his breakfast made her toes curl unexpectedly.

It didn't leave the rest of her unaffected, either.

ASIDE FROM WHEN Liam had pulled her out of the floodwaters, Whitney couldn't remember the last time she had felt this incredibly bone tired.

However, unlike that experience, this one left her feeling immensely happy, as well. She and Liam had joined the others on this Christmas tree hunt—she learned that Miss Joan chose different people for the task each year so no one monopolized the selection group by throwing their weight around. That sort of thing was strictly Miss Joan's domain alone.

It had taken a total of four hours before the group found a tree that they could all agree on, then another two to cut it down, tie it up and load it onto an oversize flatbed.

The latter was courtesy of Connie and her construction company.

It was far bigger than the one the town usually used, Liam told her. What that ultimately meant was that this year's tree was also somewhat larger than past trees. Loading it had been far from an easy matter. It was a combined effort and it had taken more than one try before they were finally successful in getting the tree onto the flatbed.

The drive back, perforce, was an exceedingly slow one.

It was, Whitney decided, like being part of a parade that was traveling its route in slow motion. They finally got back to the town square. Another hour plus was spent getting the tree off the truck and into an upright position.

"It's going a lot faster this year with all of Connie's equipment," Liam told her as she marveled at the process.

Whitney couldn't help wondering how difficult it all had to have been to accomplish *without* the aid of the construction equipment.

Yet she knew, thanks to the photographs Miss Joan had shown her earlier, that there had been a huge Christmas tree in the town square each and every year.

Because of that, and a number of other things, she found herself looking at the residents of Forever with renewed respect.

And perhaps just a touch of affection, as well.

Chapter Nine

"You *are* going to stick around to help decorate the tree, aren't you?" Miss Joan asked, materializing out of nowhere just as Whitney had begun to turn away. Liam was already walking from the town square. When she received no immediate reply, Miss Joan went on to elaborate. "I mean, after you went through all that trouble to get this beauty out here, you can't just leave it standing naked like that."

Whitney looked over her shoulder and saw that there was already a wave of people, adults and children alike, who had begun to open up boxes upon boxes of giant decorations that had been set up on more than a dozen folding tables.

Each year, according to what she had heard, more decorations were added. Last year's tree hadn't had even a single small length of branch left unadorned by at least *something*.

"From the looks of it, I'd say that you have that angle well taken care of," Whitney commented, indicating the people clustering around the laden folding tables.

"Maybe for the moment," Miss Joan allowed dismissively. "But everyone in town puts on at least a couple of decorations on the Christmas tree, if not more. It's tra—"

"—dition," Whitney completed.

As if she hadn't heard that over and over again today. To be honest, she envied the people here their traditions and their sense of community. But she was an outsider and she wasn't going to stay here long enough to be anything else.

"Yes, I know that," Whitney told the other woman.

Before she could say another word, Miss Joan took her in hand and led her over to the long row of folding tables.

"Put on a couple for me," Liam called out to her as he continued walking away. "I've got to be getting ready for work."

Whitney glanced at him in surprise. She'd just assumed that Liam would get one of his brothers to cover for him at the bar and remain here with her to decorate the tree the way Miss Joan insisted.

Obviously, he didn't feel not showing up at the bar was an option. Or maybe, after spending the better part of a day with her, Liam had had his fill.

She found that option number two bothered her. A lot. The fact that it did concerned her.

"She's in good hands," Miss Joan promised, speaking up so that her voice followed him as Liam walked away from the town square. "Don't worry, honey." Miss Joan turned her attention back to her. "I know where to find him and once you've had your fill of small-town camaraderie, I'll point you in the right direction and send you off to be with Liam."

"I wasn't worried," Whitney replied a little stiffly, feeling uncomfortable with Miss Joan's assumptions.

Had she really come across that way? Had she looked uneasy watching Liam leave? She was going to have to really work on her poker face.

Why would the older woman even *think* that? she wondered. She functioned just fine on her own. After all, she spent more than half her time being by herself, flying alone from place to place to watch young singers and bands in action, looking for that elusive, magical "something" that separated one performer or band of performers from the rest.

"Good!" Miss Joan was saying. Her voice rang with approval as the woman patted her hand. "So, let's get on with it, girl. Put a little elbow grease into it," she ordered, back to her take-charge self.

"Don't let her intimidate you," a rather tall, willowy woman with light blond hair advised.

When Whitney turned around to face this newest stranger, the woman smiled and put out her hand.

"Hi, I'm Olivia Santiago—the sheriff's wife," she added by way of introduction as Whitney shook her hand.

"Whitney Marlowe—just passing through," Whitney added in case the other woman thought otherwise.

"Between you and me, I thought Miss Joan came on like gangbusters when I first came here. The woman thought *nothing* of elbowing her way into my life. But that's just because she cares," Olivia explained. "If you ever need a friend or someone in your corner, you couldn't ask for a better person than Miss Joan," Olivia went on to assure her.

So she'd been hearing, Whitney thought. "Well, luckily, I don't need either. I don't plan on being here that long." She had no idea why that statement would make the attractive blonde smile that way. She didn't think she'd said anything funny.

Small-town residents were really rather strange people.

"Yes, that's what a lot of us said when we first found ourselves here," Olivia replied, nodding her head. And then she winked. "This is the fun part," the woman told her, leading the way over to the decorations. "C'mon, grab a few. Decorating is almost addictive."

The woman really needed to get out more. But, since she had nothing else to do at the moment—and it would appease Miss Joan—Whitney decided to take Olivia up on her invitation and joined in the initial wave of tree decorators.

WHITNEY WOUND UP staying a great deal longer than she'd intended. Not because she was forced to or found herself commandeered by Miss Joan for some other trivial task, but because she discovered, much to her amazement—and pleasure—that she was having fun.

The simple fact hadn't even dawned on her until Whitney caught herself laughing at something one of the people on her side of the tree had said in an off-handed quip.

Whitney had gotten drawn into the conversations happening around her. Before she knew it, she'd lost track of time. Not long after that, Miss Joan made the rounds, announcing that it was getting dark and decorating the remainder of the tree would resume bright and early in the morning.

"How long does decorating go on?" Whitney asked, turning to Olivia.

"Until all the decorations are on the tree and the boxes are empty," Forever's first lawyer replied.

Whitney took a couple of steps back away from the tree and looked to the uppermost part of the spruce. "How do you get the top of the tree decorated?" she asked, taking in the barren branches far above her.

"Miss Joan usually rents a cherry picker and we use that to help," Olivia told her. "This year, though, thanks to the construction project—Forever's getting its first hotel," she confided with a deep sense of town pride, "we have a cherry picker already on the premises."

That was when she realized that the woman who had befriended her didn't realize that she was currently staying in the hotel she'd just mentioned.

Whitney couldn't help smiling to herself. It was nice to know that not everyone here was like Miss Joan— ten steps ahead of her at all times.

"Did I say something funny?" Olivia asked, slightly puzzled.

"No," Whitney denied, then added quickly, "I'm just happy."

"Decorating a Christmas tree will do that to you," Olivia agreed wholeheartedly. "I think that's why Miss Joan makes such a production out of it every year. It's her personal way of spreading cheer." Olivia stopped to glance at her watch. It was obvious by her expression that what she saw was a surprise. "Look at the time. I've got to run. It was nice talking to you," she said, then asked just before she headed for home, "Are you planning on staying here awhile?"

"Couple of days at most," Whitney answered.

"A couple of days is better than nothing. Maybe I'll see you around, then," Olivia said.

"Maybe," Whitney murmured. "Oh, by the way, which way's is Murphy's?" she asked. "I got a little turned around earlier when we came back with that behemoth tree."

Olivia pointed directly behind her. "Just keep going south. You can't miss it."

Ordinarily, that was a direction that Whitney very well *could* miss. She had never had much of a sense of direction and relied completely on the GPS firmly fixed to her dashboard. Right now, it did her no good since she was separated from the device, but then this wasn't a typical crowded urban area. Forever was a small town with very little going on and if she'd been left on her own, Whitney was fairly certain she could get to the point where she had the streets—and directions for getting around in general—memorized.

As it was, even though the directions struck a familiar cord with her, it still took Whitney about ten minutes to walk from the center of town to Murphy's.

Pushing the door aside, Whitney noted that the inside of the hospitable saloon was nearly as crowded as the town square had been at the height of today's activity.

Anticipating that the crowd would only get bigger, she wove her way to the bar, expecting to find Liam behind it. After all, he had told her that he needed to work and she had just assumed that he had meant here. But instead of Liam, she saw his older brother Brett.

Had Liam lied to her? she wondered. After spending the better part of the day with her, searching for just the right Christmas tree to bring back, had he decided he had put in enough time and just wanted some space between them?

Still, she couldn't imagine Liam lying. He just didn't seem like the type to be anything but honest. Charming, yes, but still almost painfully honest.

So what, now you're making a saint out of him just because he saved you from drowning? Face it, Whit, all men are more or less alike. Their needs come first. Maybe he's already found himself someone else to occupy his time.

Maybe she had even scared him off with that kiss this morning.

Hell, she'd almost scared herself off, as well. Looking back, she had *never* felt a pull like that before—or any sort of an actual sexual pull, when she got right down to it. She hadn't had time for any sort of steady relationship, and the handful of dates she'd gone on had pretty much left her cold and convinced that the only magic to be had between a man and a woman was strictly only to be found in the movies or in some fanciful romance books.

Real life just wasn't like that.

Until it was.

With a sigh, she neatly pushed all that aside in her head and she began to turn away from the bar when she heard her name being called.

Turning around again, Whitney scanned the immediate area, curious as to who had called to her since she wasn't exactly a regular here. She sincerely doubted that any more than a handful of people even *knew* her name.

"Whitney, over here!"

That was when she saw Brett waving to her.

Once she looked in his direction, the handsome bartender beckoned her over to the section he was standing behind.

Because it would have been rude to ignore the man, Whitney forced herself to make her way through the crowd. It took a little bobbing and weaving, but she finally managed to reach him.

Once she did, Brett grinned at her. "I see you survived Miss Joan's annual Christmas tree foraging."

She survived, all right, but there were times when she felt as if she had just barely succeeded. "She certainly is something else," Whitney replied evasively.

In total agreement, Brett was nodding his head. "The woman does take a little getting used to," he replied. "It helps to know that her heart's in the right place."

"So people keep telling me," Whitney commented. But that just wasn't enough of a recommendation to her. And then, because she felt she didn't have anything to lose—after all, she would be leaving town the minute her car was repaired, which meant that she'd never see any of these people again—that was her incentive to ask Brett, "Is Liam around? I thought he'd be tending the bar, but obviously, he's not."

"Liam doesn't tend bar very much anymore. His interests have taken him in a new, different direction," Brett said.

As he continued speaking to her, Brett took a rather impressive-looking bottle from the rear counter. It was filled with a thick amber liquid. He poured a very small amount into a shot glass. Placing the bottle back on the display behind him, he moved the shot glass closer to Whitney.

"First one's on the house," he told her with a warm smile.

Rather than reach for it, Whitney eyed the drink for a moment.

"What is it?" she asked.

"Nothing lethal," Brett promised. "Just a little something to take the chill out of your bones—it is December 1, after all, even if we don't have snow around here."

There was no real chill as far as she was concerned, but she took a tentative sip from her glass. As the liquid made its way through her system she raised her eyes to his.

"Bénédictine?" she asked.

Brett appeared impressed. "Ah, the lady has a discerning palate," he declared with a note of admiration.

"A lot of the deals I make are closed over drinks," she explained. "Some of the people tend to favor Bénédictine, which is how I know what it tastes like."

Pausing for a moment, she contemplated the remaining contents of her glass. "These interests that Liam has developed," she began, getting back to what Brett had said to her a minute ago, "just which way are they taking him?"

"Well, if he's good enough, probably the sky's the limit," Brett guessed, and then as he looked at her, he went on to add, "But then, you'd be the better judge of that than I would."

A third sip had her finishing the drink he had placed in front of her. Whitney put the shot glass back on the bar and her eyes met his. What he'd just said clearly intrigued her.

"How's that?" She was completely in the dark about what he was talking about.

Brett tried to explain it another way. "It's an area that you're far more familiar with than I am."

He wasn't making any sense to her. She looked down at the shot glass. "That was only one shot and I can pretty much hold my liquor, so it's not the alcohol making my brain fuzzy. But I don't understand what you're talking about," she freely admitted.

Brett, like his brother Liam, had that going for him. Charming, he had a way of dismantling barriers, dismantling them in such a way that one minute they were there, the next, they were gone and life had taken on a far more meaningful, far more satisfactory air.

"Why would I be the better judge than you?"

Rather than answer her question outright, Brett smiled and refilled her glass, pouring from the same bottle.

"That's okay," she said. "I don't need another." Though two drinks still didn't make her unsteady, she didn't see the need to stand there essentially drinking by herself. That was for people trying to erase something from their memory.

"I'm thinking that maybe, this one time, you just might need a second one."

They really did talk in riddles in this town, she thought, frustrated. They should all come with an instruction manual.

Maybe this penchant for riddles had something to do with the fact that there seemed to be preciously little entertainment to be had in Forever. Outside of the saloon, she hadn't seen anything that promised to cut into the day-to-day, wall-to-wall boredom.

There were no malls, small or otherwise—there wasn't even so much as one mini-mall. There were no chain movie theaters. From what she could ascertain, there wasn't even *one* movie theater in the entire town. There certainly wasn't a restaurant to challenge Miss Joan's diner for business.

There was, in effect, nothing that served as some sort of a temporary diversion for the people of this small town.

So, poking their noses into other people's business and saying enigmatic statements that made little to no sense to an outsider seemed to be the residents' only means to entertain themselves.

She looked at the refilled shot glass with its shimmering contents. "Well, I'm just going to leave it where it is, but since you poured it, it can't go back into the bottle. So let me pay you for it. That way, it doesn't count as a loss to you.

"Tell Liam the excursion earlier was really an experience." She paused a second, then added, "Tell him I really had fun."

There was no harm in telling the man the truth, especially if she didn't see him again.

Then Brett said something that blew that out of the water for her.

"Why don't you tell him yourself?"

"I would if I could," she told Brett, "but since he's not around—"

Brett interrupted her again. "Turn around," he said. When she went on staring at him, confusion creasing her brow, Brett pointed behind her.

It was so noisy in here, with people shouting over one another to be heard, she had a hard time hearing

Brett, and the bartender was standing just a couple of feet away from her.

Still deliberately leaving her drink on the bar, Whitney turned around just as she heard someone—was that Liam?—loudly counting off, "Three, two, one!"

The next second, the countdown was instantly followed by a rather enthusiastic burst of music she could literally feel into her very bones.

That was certainly an attention getter.

It had certainly gotten hers.

By the time Whitney had managed to turn all the way around, she noticed a four-piece band set up some distance from the middle of the saloon.

There was a man playing an upright keyboard, accompanying three guitarists. The one in the middle was the only one who was singing.

The one in the middle was also Liam.

Like someone in a trance, Whitney, her eyes riveted on the band, slowly reached behind her for the drink that she had just rejected. She spread her fingers out, trying to make contact with the shot glass.

Taking pity on her, Brett pushed the shot glass into her questing fingers. Triumphantly securing it, Whitney brought the shot glass to her, then raised it in a single toast to the band.

The drink disappeared in one gulp.

Chapter Ten

"Would you like another?" Brett asked, his amusement plainly audible.

He addressed the words to the back of Whitney's head. She was on the bar stool, sitting absolutely ram-rod straight. Every fiber in her body was focused on the band. More specifically, on Liam.

"I'll let you know," she finally told Brett after a beat, the words all but dribbling from her lips in slow motion.

"All right," Brett answered.

Even those words were too many, interfering with her concentration. Whitney waved him into silence, wishing she could do that with the rest of the people who were in the saloon. She was doing her best to try to hear the song the band was playing, really hear it. She wanted to be sure she wasn't mistaken, or talking herself into something.

But even the surrounding chatter couldn't diminish or detract from what she knew she was hearing: one rather professional-sounding band playing background for one extremely excellent-singing guitarist.

She became even *more* impressed when Liam indulged in some entertaining, albeit exceedingly difficult, guitar fingering.

Sliding off the bar stool she'd only been partially perched on, Whitney abandoned her place by the bar and came closer to the music, drawn there more or less like one of the hypnotized children mesmerized by the Pied Piper's flute.

She stopped herself just a little short of the perimeter that surrounded the band.

As she absorbed the quality of the music, she began to notice other equally as important things, as well. Such as the fact that the inner circle that surrounded the band was comprised predominately of young women. Young women who appeared to be absolutely spellbound, hanging on every syllable Liam sang, on every note he played.

There were men in the outer circle that went around the band, but the band appealed in no small way predominately to the female of the species. Whitney wasn't sure how she felt about this, but for the moment, she was excited by what she saw.

WHENEVER HE PLAYED, whether to an audience or just in rehearsal, where only the other band members were present, Liam always gave 150 percent of himself to the performance.

But tonight, he'd kept just a fraction of himself back in order to aim a covert glance or two in Whitney's direction. He wanted to impress her. To literally wow her.

He told himself it was because of who she was and ultimately who she represented. After all, she was a talent scout for a major recording label.

But while that was all very true, it wasn't the only

reason he wanted to blow Whitney away with his dex- terity and with his musical prowess.

At bottom lay the reason that all men flexed what- ever muscles they had available—be it physical or mental—to impress the ladies in their lives.

When he finally got himself to glance up, he saw her. Saw Whitney. Saw her swaying to the beat of the song they were playing.

That she was standing closer rather than lingering by the bar gave him a very positive feeling, not to men- tion what it did for his confidence.

Liam deliberately made eye contact with her now and while that sort of thing was supposed to make a huge impression on the recipient of his gaze, he found to his surprise that making eye contact with Whitney also sent a shaft of heat through him.

At the very same time, he felt a shiver work its way down his back. He was behaving like some damn fool teenager. It was a good thing that Whitney wasn't into mind reading or his goose would have *really* been cooked.

Because she did look so captivated, Liam went straight into the next number without pausing when he and the band concluded the one they had been playing.

They wound up doing five numbers that way. At the end of the fifth number, Liam took command of the microphone set up in the center.

"The guys and I are going to give our fingers a little rest by taking a short break," he announced. "But don't go away too far 'cause the show's going to resume in a few minutes. Until then, drink up!" he ordered with an infectious grin. With that, he returned the mike back to its stand and stepped away from the makeshift stage Finn had put together for them.

Several of the band's—and his—would-be groupies immediately converged, blocking his path as he tried to make his way over toward Whitney. Gently but firmly, he got the young women to get out of his way.

"So?" Liam asked with enthusiasm the second he reached her. "What do you think?"

He was all but radiating pure sex appeal, Whitney thought, struggling to see him objectively rather than as the young performer whose unorchestrated kiss had completely rocked the very foundations of her world.

"I think," she replied, "you should have told me that you can sing."

He laughed shortly. "You mean I left that off my résumé when I handed it to you?" he asked, acting surprised at the omission.

Whitney's eyes narrowed. Had she overlooked something? "What résumé?"

Liam's expression bordered on triumphant. He'd made his point, or so he thought. "Exactly."

"Wait, back up," Whitney ordered. This was *not* making any sense to her. If she had been in his place when this situation had arose, she would have lost absolutely *no* time making her musical bent known to him. "When I told you that I was a talent scout for Purely Platinum, that didn't ring any bells for you?"

Again, he laughed. If she only knew the kind of restraint he'd employed to keep from telling her about his aspirations for himself and his band.

"It rang an entire wind-chimes factory full of them for me," he told her.

She stared at him, getting more and more confused.

"Then *why* didn't you tell me you were in a band and that you were a damn good singer?"

"And musician," Brett added, having rounded the bar for a moment to come over and join Whitney and his brother. When she looked at him over her shoulder, Brett went on to explain. "Liam also wrote most of the songs the band's playing tonight."

"Really?" She turned and directed her question at Liam.

If she'd had anywhere near the talent she had just witnessed, she would have been out performing her heart out in every venue she could find until someone discovered her—the way she had just discovered Liam and his band right now. Excitement surged through her veins.

Whitney watched now as a boyish flush washed over Liam's ultra-handsome chiseled features. He nodded his head almost as an afterthought, blond hair slipping over his eyes. He combed it back with his fingers and looked at her.

"Yeah, I wrote them. No big deal," he murmured with a vague, dismissive shrug.

"Yes, big deal," she contradicted. "You should have said *something*."

"Couldn't take the chance that it would have sounded like bragging to you. So I figured it would come across better if you heard us play," he said, explaining his reasoning as best he could. "I mean, you probably get a lot of people telling you they've always wanted to play or sing professionally and that all their friends tell them how good they are—even if they sound like fingernails scraping across a chalkboard. I didn't want you to think I was in that group."

"Then what are you saying? That you don't want to play professionally?"

He looked at her as if she'd lost her mind. "Oh, yeah, sure we want to play professionally. That's what our goal is—the band's and mine," he elaborated, nodding toward the other three members of his band, who weren't quite as fast or as good as he was when it came to avoiding overly energetic fans. "But you probably get a lot of people saying that and you probably have a way to block them all out. I didn't want you ruling the band out just because you're tired of every second person thinking they could be the next big sensation on the entertainment scene."

He was right, she realized. She would have probably dismissed him out of hand if he'd come across the standard way. It had become second nature for her, a way of preserving herself. Whenever people learned what she did for a living, they suddenly began singing under their breath rather loudly, or tapping out tunes to direct her attention to them.

Consequently, Liam had gone about it just the right way, she couldn't help thinking. Not only had he gotten her to listen, but he'd also turned out to be damn good. Ordinarily, the label she represented didn't have—nor had it ever had—a country-and-western performer in their stable. Purely Platinum focused predominantly on contemporary pop stars—but good was good, she thought. And Liam and his band were *damn* good.

About to say something else to her, Liam seemed to catch a movement out of the corner of his eye. When he turned to look, he must have seen one of the remaining guitarists beckoning for him to come back. Their first break was over and it was time to begin a second set.

"Music calls," he told Whitney just before he started making his way back to the band.

An equal number of girls—if not more—impeded his route back, getting in his way, asking for autographs or just simply fawning over him.

Whitney certainly didn't blame them. Liam was nothing if not incredibly appealing. He didn't even need to sing to knock them dead.

"Seeing those girls acting like that, you'd never know that they all went to school with Liam," Brett commented to her, watching his youngest brother.

"It's the performer phenomenon," Whitney told him knowingly.

"The what?" he asked her.

"The performer phenomenon," she repeated, then explained what she meant. "Doesn't matter if they grew up living next door to one another and playing together in a sandbox every day for fifteen years," Whitney exaggerated. "You stick an instrument in one of their hands, shine a spotlight on them—or a big flashlight— and make them sing, provided that they *can* sing even a little," she stipulated, "and suddenly, his lifelong neighbor is seeing him with new eyes and getting giddy, thanks to fantasies that are materializing in her head. It's like he's changed into some kind of a minigod right before her eyes. Trust me, I've seen it happen again and again."

She paused, listening to the newest number Liam and his band were playing. "Excuse me for a second," she said to Brett, searching for her phone.

"No problem," he said. He shouldn't have taken this long of a break himself. "I've got to get back to the bar.

Finn can only stand filling orders for so long before he gets antsy," Brett told her with a laugh.

She barely nodded to acknowledge that she'd heard him. Her mind was on capturing Liam's performance while she could.

Her smartphone in hand, Whitney pulled up her video app. Pressing it, she then aimed her phone at Liam and began recording him as he sang and played.

Still watching Liam, she smiled to herself. "Have I got a surprise for you, big brother," she murmured under her breath, suddenly exceedingly pleased with herself. "Looks like almost drowning turned out to be a good thing."

What was it her mother used to say, she tried to recall. Something about nothing bad ever happening that some good couldn't come of it.

This was definitely a good thing.

Her almost drowning and subsequently getting stranded out here in nowhere land turned out to be definitely a good thing because if that hadn't happened to her, if she hadn't gotten swept up in that awful flash flood, she wouldn't be here now, listening to what could very well be Purely Platinum's latest superstars.

She went on taping.

ONCE AGAIN, LIAM came over to her during his next break. He was flushed, having worked up a real sweat this time out, but he was also obviously very pleased with himself.

He and the band had outdone themselves, Liam felt—and he was usually his own worst critic. But tonight, tonight they had played as if a fleet of angels had pulled up a cloud to listen to them and they in turn had given it their all.

It didn't hurt that he had told the band who Whitney was and the label she was with.

"Why the hell didn't you tell us?" Sam had demanded, stunned.

"I didn't want to make you nervous," Liam had answered.

The other three performers had been far from happy with the answer, but they *were* grateful for the opportunity now.

They had played their hearts out.

"How is it that you're still here, playing in a saloon in Forever?" Whitney asked Liam the moment he joined her.

That was a simple enough question to answer. He'd stayed up until now because he'd honed his skills here. "Because Brett lets me try out new songs here and besides, this is where the guys and I got started. It's home to us."

She understood the appeal of home. Home, for her, had been her mother. But then everything had changed when she had abandoned the family in favor of a man a lot younger than her. Now, to her, home was someplace to leave.

"Home's a nice place to come back to when you need to rest up," she said for Liam's sake, "but, well, haven't you ever wanted to go out on the road, play to different audiences, make money—no, make a *living* at this?" she pressed.

As she asked the question, a thought hit her. "Does Brett even pay you for playing here?" she asked, fairly certain she knew the answer to that before Liam said it.

Loyalty had Liam carefully gauging his answer.

"Not at first," he admitted, "but that was because we were just starting out, developing our skills, our pacing, things like that. But he pays us now," he said, then, because Brett was such a stickler for the truth and had all but drummed it into his head as well as Finn's, he added, "Or at least he pays the guys."

"But not you?" she asked incredulously. "You're the singer." *And the real reason there are so many females packing the place tonight,* Whitney added silently.

"And related to the owners—not to mention that I'm also one of the owners," he reminded her. "Seems kind of silly to be paying myself."

"It seems even 'sillier' to do it for free," Whitney deliberately countered. "It's like throwing away a precious commodity."

"Precious, huh?" Liam repeated with a very wide grin. A grin that was swiftly getting under her skin. She could see why the other women reacted the way they did to Liam. The man was *very* hard to resist. "Is that what you really think?"

"Absolutely," she told him, doing her best to sound professional and distant.

She was only partially successful.

Clearing her throat, she continued, "I've been in the business for practically ten years now and you are one of the best—if not *the* best—performer that I have ever heard."

Liam was one to always hammer things down and put them into perspective. He'd grown confident over the past year, confident, but not cocky. The latter was the road to self-destruction in his opinion and he intended to be around, playing or doing whatever it was he liked, for a very long time.

"You're just saying that because I saved your life," he said with a grin.

"No," she contradicted quite seriously, "I'm saying that because it's true."

Liam couldn't keep the wide smile from his face. He was fairly beaming inside. It was one thing to have one of the locals rave about the band and tell him how good they—and he—were. Hearing that was good for the soul. But having someone of Whitney's caliber, someone who did this sort of thing for a living, tell him he was good was an entirely different matter.

Her words had him walking on air.

Impulsively, Liam turned around and waved for his band to join them.

"Hey, guys," he called out. "Come over here. Remember what I told you? Well, I think it's time for you all to meet." He paused to look at Whitney for a second. "You don't mind, do you?" he asked her, realizing that he'd taken her assent for granted.

"No, I don't mind," she replied. "I'd really like to meet them."

"Great!" he said with genuine feeling.

Turning, Liam beckoned to them again, this time with enthusiastic hand movements. The other members of the band made their way over to Liam and the woman he was talking to.

"Whitney, I'd like you to meet Sam Howard, Christian Grey Eagle and Tom Grant. Guys, this is Whitney Marlowe. She's the talent scout for Purely Platinum recording studio I told you about. She's auditioning singers and musicians."

Sam Howard had deep blue-black hair that was straighter than a pin. He was tall, with cheekbones that seemed to have been carved out of ivory and at the moment, his dark, chocolate-colored eyes were scrutinizing her.

"Did you like what you heard?" he asked Whitney point-blank.

"Very much so," she told the man. "I think your band has a great deal of energy that is extremely infectious. You make the audience part of your music."

Whitney didn't add that it had been a very long time since she had been this impressed with a band. But they were new and fresh and listening to them was an exciting experience.

She had a feeling that Wilson would agree with her—after, of course, he finished being dismissive and complaining that they were too raw and that they sang country, of all things. Then he'd tell her that the publicity department didn't have a clue as to how to promote county-and-western music or performers who specialized in that genre.

But in the end, she was certain that he would come around and grudgingly mutter that yes, they did have a lot of potential.

Because, Whitney thought as she watched Liam go back to the makeshift stage and pick up his guitar again, the band certainly did have potential—a great deal of potential.

They began to play again and Whitney felt herself completely transported. Within seconds, she began taping again.

Chapter Eleven

"You really think we're good?" Liam asked her later on that night as he drove Whitney back to the hotel. Nature had slipped into a respectful stillness while the full moon illuminated the road before them, guiding them on their way. "I'm not asking for myself," he interjected quickly before she had a chance to answer him. He didn't want Whitney to think he was so shallow he would get her to stroke his ego. He had a logical reason for asking about her opinion. "I just don't want to raise the guys' hopes if you're just being nice. We've been at this a long time and the band's really important to us."

"Yes," she answered him with a smile, "I think you're not just good but *very* good. I think with the right person to manage you, you'll go far."

Liam parked his truck in front of the hotel and got out.

"The right person," Liam repeated slowly as if rolling the matter over in his head to come to a conclusion. "You?"

Whitney blinked, surprised as she got out of the passenger side of the vehicle. "What? No, not me." She hadn't meant to imply that. She was just speaking in general terms. "I just find talent. You need an agent, a manager, someone to look out for you, book you in the right places. Someone with business savvy, the patience of Job and a good ear," she told him as he walked her to the hotel's entrance.

Liam stopped walking just inside the hotel lobby and shifted the lantern he was holding to his other hand. He was confused.

"Well, isn't that you?" he asked. "I think you just described what you do."

"Maybe in a general sort of way," she granted. "But you need more than just what I do as you get started building a career."

"What the band and I need," he pointed out, "is someone we can trust. Someone we feel has our best interests at heart." He was looking straight at her as he put forth his band's requirement for the future.

She had to admit that the idea of representing Liam and his band was tempting. She'd only been at the very beginning of a couple of performers' careers, but even then it had been strictly in a distant, advisory capacity. The way she viewed it, she wasn't cutthroat enough to be a successful agent.

"Look, Liam," she began, "I'm flattered, but you need someone with a lot more expertise than I have." She thought for a second, then went on. "I've got a list of agents somewhere. Why don't I—"

"Maybe I don't want someone with more expertise than you," Liam said, not letting her finish what she was saying. "Maybe I want someone who's as hungry as I am to get somewhere in that particular field, hungry to get started in this business and build a career."

Oh, dear God, Whitney thought as she looked up at

him, she was tempted. Really, *really* tempted. What Liam was suggesting—managing his band—would be taking a chance. It meant challenging herself, taking a real risk by leaving everything she knew behind and starting fresh in a brand-new, virgin world. It would mean giving up her comfort zone and the perks she had right now and diving headfirst into the deep end of the pool.

What perks? A little voice in her head jeered. *You spend half the year traveling around, sleeping in strange, uncomfortable hotel beds, periodically calling Wilson and arguing with him until he comes around. That's not a life. That's an existence. When you think about it, maybe it's even a rut.*

Still, rut or not, it was *her* rut and she could depend on it.

"Tell you what, Liam, why don't we just take this whole idea one step at a time? Is that okay with you?" she asked.

Liam nodded, the moonlight outlining his chiseled features and managing somehow to make them even sexier than they already were. If the man looked any sexier, Whitney caught herself thinking, there would probably be a law on the books requiring him to wear a paper bag over his head in public. As it was, she could hardly keep from running her fingers through his light blond hair. It looked silky—was it? she wondered.

"Okay," Liam agreed to her suggestion.

Arriving at her door, he put the lantern down on the floor.

The next moment, rather than opening the door for her, Liam managed to surprise her by slipping his fingers into her hair and framing her face.

Whitney could feel her heart starting to accelerate, beating hard with an anticipation she really shouldn't be having, she silently lectured herself.

But she made no move to put distance between herself and Liam. Instead, she asked him in a voice that was hardly above a whisper, "What are you doing?"

"I'm just following your suggestion," he told her, his face so serious Whitney had no idea just what she was to expect.

Everything inside of her was on edge, anticipation all but overwhelming her. "My suggestion?"

Liam nodded his head. Light blond hair fell into his eyes but he ignored it. His gaze never left hers. "Taking it one step at a time."

And then, with the moonlight pushing its way in through the various windows, wrapping itself around them, Liam drew her a fraction of an inch closer, lowered his mouth to hers and kissed her.

Unlike the first time they'd kissed, this kiss began slowly, softly, but with a purpose. Even though it flowered at an even pace, it drew all the energy from her in a single instant. She came close to melting away in the ensuing wave of heat.

One moment, the kiss was so gentle, so delicate, it felt as light as a butterfly's wing fluttering by. The next moment, heated passion all but exploded between them and for the life of her, she couldn't tell if he was the one who had struck the match—or if she was. All she knew was that something far more powerful than she had taken over, all but consuming her with its head-spinning majesty.

This was wrong, wrong, wrong. Her brain kept telegraphing the protest to the rest of her, desperately trying to get the message registered and acted on.

Allowing what was taking place to go any further was wrong for so many reasons, it was difficult to know where to begin. She was mixing business with pleasure, interweaving her professional life with her private one and worse than that, she was behaving like a cougar in training, or maybe just a plain, old-fashioned cradle robber.

And her resolve was growing weaker by the moment.

But as much as she could so very easily succumb to what was happening to her, Whitney summoned every last ounce of strength she still had and separated her mouth from his.

She saw the bewilderment, the question in Liam's eyes, and knew she couldn't just turn her back on him and walk off. She had to explain, to make him see *why* she couldn't allow this to happen between them.

She began with the most basic of reasons why they shouldn't sleep together—because she knew that was where this was clearly headed. "How old are you?"

Liam stared at her, a look of bewilderment on his face that made her rethink her question.

"What's my age have to do with anything?"

"A lot," she insisted, her eyes narrowing to tiny laser points focused on him. "Now, how old are you?" she repeated.

"Old enough," Liam maintained.

That's what people said when they *weren't* old enough. "Well, I'm older."

He nodded his head as if to evaluate her. "And I

see that you're getting around just fine without your walker," he cracked.

That managed to get her more annoyed. "I'm not making jokes," she snapped.

"You're also not making sense," Liam countered calmly.

"Don't you understand? I'm *older* than you," Whitney informed him pointedly, certain of the fact now.

Liam shrugged, completely unmoved by this so-called revelation. "A lot of people are. So what?"

"So it bothers *me*," she insisted hotly. There were so many ugly names for the situation she found herself almost entangled in. She wanted to nip this right in the bud. It couldn't be allowed to flower.

Again Liam lifted his broad shoulders in a careless shrug. "It doesn't bother me," he said.

How could it not? she wondered. "It should," she told him in no uncertain terms, implying that if it didn't bother him, then there was something wrong with the way he was thinking.

"Why?" Liam pressed. "You're a beautiful woman who has sophistication and maturity on her side. If anything, you're like a fine wine, although I doubt you've had much time to ferment," he teased, softly kissing her temples one at a time.

Liam was definitely making it exceedingly difficult to resist him, but she knew she had to. Had to keep a clear head and not succumb to the havoc Liam was creating inside of her. If for no other reason, she had to keep him at arm's length to prevent Wilson from accusing her of pushing a personal agenda by getting him to watch Liam perform. Wilson was very quick to label things. Nepotism was Wilson's favorite thing to rail against, despite the fact that he was guilty of it himself time and again.

"I'm twenty-seven," Liam said. "How old are you?"

Twenty-seven. She was almost four years older than that. Four whole years. Practically half a decade. However, she wasn't ready to admit any of it. "More than twenty-seven."

Very slowly, his eyes swept over the length of her, lingering a little during the passage. "I'm willing to bet it's not much more. One year? Two? Six?"

"Six?" she cried, her eyes widening in apparent shock and dismay. And then she realized by Liam's grin that he had somehow set her up—to what end?

"Okay," he said and nodded, taking in every nuance that had just transpired between Whitney and himself. "More than two and, judging by that cry, less than six. So that means that you've got a few years left before you forget how to feed yourself and have to be shipped off to a nursing home. I suggest you enjoy them."

"I am," she informed him with a toss of her head. It was a studied move, but she felt it did the trick. "I'm doing what I like. I'm discovering new talent."

"Commendable," Liam wholeheartedly agreed. "But how about discovering yourself?"

What was that supposed to mean? "I don't have to discover myself. I know just who I am," she told him. "I always have."

She found his smile to be positively wicked and incredibly disarming even if she struggled to give no indication of that.

"Yeah," Liam agreed to her assessment. "The lady who can make me forget just about everything else," he told her and just to show her what he meant by that, he kissed her again.

This time the gentleness was placed on hold, allowing the passion to come out in full force. So much so that she was swept away. She had to throw her arms around his neck just to anchor herself to something.

The kiss continued to grow in what amounted to a matter of seconds.

At that point Whitney realized that she was ready to throw caution, principles and everything in between into the wind in exchange for something intangible, but incredibly wonderful—even though it was fleeting and unpredictable.

Most likely, she would have done just that, had Liam not stopped what was happening when he did.

Just as Whitney was ready to lose herself in him, Liam stepped back, smiled into her eyes and said, "Pleasant dreams."

She didn't know whether to throw something at him, drag him to her room or just run for cover as fast as she could.

She walked sedately for cover instead just as Liam walked back to his truck.

He had absolutely no idea just how frustrated she was.

WHITNEY WAS FAR too keyed up to go to bed—not that she had expected to get too much sleep that night.

Once she returned to her hotel room, her initial plan was to begin editing the videos she had taken of Liam and his band with her cell phone. Not altogether certain how long the process would take, she had meant only to get started.

But whenever she got caught up in something, it became a matter of putting going to bed off for an extra ten minutes, just until she completed work on the next frame and then the next one. Telling herself that all she wanted to do was make a little tweak here, a slightly larger tweak there, and so on.

Then, before she knew it, daylight slipped into her room, dueling with the light from the lantern left on in the suite.

She didn't take immediate note of even *that*. She realized it was the dawn of a new day somewhat after the fact.

Whitney glanced at her watch and blinked. That couldn't be true. Yet as she looked at the old-fashioned face, she saw that it was close to eight o'clock.

She had been up all night.

But she had also done some pretty impressive editing, she realized and congratulated herself. The editing had included finding a way to filter out the noisy, albeit appreciative, patrons who had surrounded the band. The only time she allowed the noisy crowd was to highlight the band's strengths as well as its strong appeal.

The rest of the time, she made sure that the band's sound was the dominant one on the video file.

"Okay, Wilson," she said, addressing the air, "prepare to have your socks knocked off, starting from all the way up to your knees."

She played the video for herself one more time to make sure everything was as perfect as she could get it—then she pressed Send and forwarded the video she had spent all night editing to her brother.

Drained and exhilarated at the same time, Whitney

decided that a shower was in order. So she allowed herself only three extra minutes to absorb the hot water beating down on her rigid shoulders and body.

The shower, seductive in its heat, went on a little longer before she finally turned the faucet off and stepped out of the stall. Toweling herself off, she got dressed quickly, then, after a few seconds of psyching herself up, placed a call to Wilson.

Her brother's phone rang four times on his end before she heard it finally going to voice mail. Her hand tightened on her own phone.

"Pick up, Wilson, you'll thank me when you do." She gave it to the count of twenty, then placed another call to him.

And another.

By her count, she placed twelve calls in all before her brother finally picked up his phone and answered it none-too-politely.

"What?" Wilson fairly roared into the phone. "Are you completely insane, Whit? Should I start calling you Half-Whit?"

"Whitney is just fine," she informed her brother crisply. "And, for the record, I'm not insane, just persistent," she replied, her voice softening slightly. "Remember, that's part of my charm."

"You don't have any charm," Wilson snapped at her. "Especially not at six in the morning."

"It's not six," Whitney informed her older brother.

"It is here," he said coldly.

"It *was*," she corrected. She'd forgotten about the time difference, she realized. But she wasn't *that* far off and besides, she wanted to talk to him about Liam and his band. "It's later now—and anyway, when I'm finished telling you why I called, you're going to thank me and want to know why I didn't call you earlier."

"Ha!" He laughed as if *that* would be the day. "Did you by any chance come down with something in that hick town you're staying in? The cattle don't have anthrax, do they?" he jeered.

"I haven't seen any cattle and I haven't come down with anything," she said. "I've just been doing my job."

He took that to mean only one thing. "You auditioned The Lonely Wolves?" he asked, apparently coming to life on the other end of the line. "I thought you said they were short a drummer."

"No, I didn't audition *that* group. But I found a group that's even better than they are," she told him, not bothering to bridle her enthusiasm.

"How would you know that? You just said that you haven't auditioned The Lonely Wolves yet, right?" Wilson asked smugly, obviously tickled to have caught her in a lie.

"Right, but we do have that demo they sent, so I think it's safe to say the group I heard last night is twice— if not three times—as good as the one you sent me to audition."

"I'm getting confused here," her brother grumbled. "Are you saying—"

She had no patience to engage in lengthy explanations for the sake of clearing up her brother's apparently foggy brain. Instead, she cut him off and made another suggestion.

"Put me on hold and watch the video I sent you," she said. "I'll wait."

Wilson snorted in disgust. "I'll call you back later."

She knew that meant he was going back to bed and

she wanted him to watch the video first. "No, I'll wait," she insisted.

He was obviously out of patience, something he never had a large supply of to begin with. "If I fired you, would you go away?"

"Nope. And you can't fire me," she reminded him. "I'm part owner, remember?"

"All too well," he complained. "Okay, I'll watch your stupid video—but if I don't like it, that's the end of it, okay?"

"If you don't like it," she told him, "then I'd seriously think about having you committed because it'll mean you've lost your taste as well as your business savvy."

"What I'd really like to lose is you," Wilson snapped back.

"Maybe someday, but not now. Now go watch the video," she ordered. "I'll be right here when you're done." Provided, of course, that her brother didn't hit the wrong key, as he was wont to do, and disconnect them.

The next minute, she had dead air registering against her ear, which could, but didn't necessarily have to, mean that she had been disconnected.

With a sigh, she told herself it was an accident on Wilson's part. There was a fifty-fifty chance that it was just that. But, knowing her older brother's pigheaded approach to certain things, like being woken up at an early hour, she was inclined to believe that he'd just ended the call and hoped she'd go away.

"Think again, Will," she declared, punching in his number again on her keypad.

Chapter Twelve

It took her three more tries before she got Wilson to pick up his phone and talk to her again. The first two attempts wound up ringing five times, then going to voice mail. Once she heard the prerecorded message beginning, she'd terminate her call and then hit Redial to start the process all over again.

Whitney was prepared to continue redialing until she wore him down, or he threw out his phone, whichever came first.

When he finally got back on the phone, Wilson was *not* a happy camper. "I swear I'm going to take out a restraining order against you," he declared in a voice that was barely below shouting range.

"A restraining order against your own sister and business partner? I really don't think you'll be able to get one. The judge'll see this as a family matter and tell you to sit down and talk to me—which is what I want in the first place," she informed her brother cheerfully. "Now, stop being so stubborn and take a look at that video I just sent you. Trust me, you'll be glad you did." She knew he hated it when she took the lead, but this time it was justified. She honestly thought that Liam and his band had that something extra that set them apart from the crowd.

She heard Wilson blowing out a beleaguered breath and knew that he was slowly coming around. "Just where did you find this band you're so hot about?"

"I heard them last night right here at the local saloon," Whitney replied.

"Where's 'here'?" Wilson asked. She could almost see him frowning as he spoke. It took a great deal to make Wilson smile.

She answered his question. "The town's name is Forever."

Wilson snorted dismissively. "Never heard of it." It was impossible to miss the superior tone in his voice.

"The town's name isn't important, Will," she insisted, beginning to lose patience with her brother. "Just watch the video."

She was surprised that Wilson's sigh didn't blow her away, it was that deep, that put-upon.

"Okay, okay, just as long as I'm not listening to a country-western band," he said. When she made no comment—or offered any reassurances—she heard her brother groan audibly. "Oh, God, please tell me that you didn't send me a video of a country-western group."

"Would you please just watch the video—and keep an open mind," she ordered.

He didn't seem to have heard her, but was marching to his own inner tune. "It is, isn't it?" Wilson demanded. "It's some two-bit country-western band made up of three dimwits who have trouble remembering which end of the guitar to play and some guy who yodels, right? Whit, you know damn well that we don't have any crying-in-your-beer groups under contract. We never have and we never will."

"Never say never," Whitney countered. "You just might have to eat your own words. Besides," she continued in defense of the group she'd been instantly impressed with, "they're not crying into their beer or into anything else. Now watch the damn video. I've got a feeling that if we don't sign these people, we're really going to regret it—and that's not how this business works."

Wilson's voice took on an edge—she knew he didn't like her lecturing him, but she was out of options. "I'm already filled with regret," Wilson grumbled.

"Wilson…" she began, a warning note in her voice, although, quite honestly, she wasn't sure what more she could threaten her brother with if he decided to stand firm.

There was a long pause on the other end of the line. And then, in a far less adversarial tone, Wilson asked, "You're really serious about this band, aren't you, Whitney?"

Finally, he was getting the message, she thought, relieved. "Yes."

"And you want to sign this band even if we've never put country singers under contract, not even so much as once."

"Yes, I do," she replied unwaveringly.

"Well, if you're that gung ho about it, the least I can do is give this video of yours a look-see," he agreed, relenting. "Stand by," he instructed. "I'll get back to you when it's over." He proceeded to put her on hold, this time successfully.

The video she had sent him included three songs,

bringing the playing time in at just a shade over ten minutes. She marked that down on her watch and proceeded to wait.

They were, she judged, quite possibly the *longest* ten minutes of her life.

Her shoulder and arm slowly began to ache from holding the cell phone by her head. Even so, she didn't dare put the phone down. She could very well miss her brother's feedback when he returned to the call. She knew the way Wilson operated. If she didn't answer immediately, he would just hang up and move on to something else. This was already hard enough. Convincing her brother to give her—and Liam's band—a second chance was in the same category as walking on water: it was done just once in history and was not about to happen again.

She was beginning to think that Wilson had decided to leave her on hold when she finally heard sounds on the other end of the line. The next second, she heard her brother's voice.

"You filmed this?"

"With my own little hands," she cracked, then became serious. "The band's good, isn't it?" she asked with a certain amount of pride.

Rather than agree with her, her brother allowed, "The singer's got some potential."

"Some?" Whitney echoed incredulously. Was Wilson kidding? Or was it just hard for her brother to give her any credit for finding a really good band? "Pretend it's not me you're talking to. Pretend the video came from one of your other talent scouts."

Again she heard Wilson sigh. She held her breath,

waiting. "Okay, more than some. How soon can you get this guy out here? I want to hear him for myself."

She had her doubts about Liam and his band dropping everything and flying out to Los Angeles at a moment's notice. From what she'd observed, that wasn't the way things seemed to operate around here.

"Well, if you want the full Forever Band experience, I think you're going to have to come out here and listen to them play in surroundings they're comfortable with."

Wilson snorted, clearly insulted. "In what scenario does the mountain come to Mohammed?"

"In the scenario where the mountain wants to make money," she replied calmly.

There was silence again on the other end and she knew Wilson was weighing his options—his pride versus his business acumen. When he spoke again, she had a feeling that the acumen had gotten the upper hand. "I'll look at my schedule and get back to you later today," Wilson told her. "How about you? You leaving this hole-in-the-wall anytime soon?" he asked. "Or do they have you chained in someone's basement?"

"No chains," she said simply. "My car's not ready yet. The mechanic's having trouble getting the parts that are needed."

"Take it to another mechanic," he advised.

"There is no other mechanic in this town," she told him.

"Huh." The sound was exceedingly dismissive and pregnant with covert meaning. "You ask me, you're being played."

Ah, but I didn't ask you, did I?

Whitney knew better than to say that out loud. It

would only get Wilson's back up and send him off on yet another round of lectures.

"Thanks for the input, Will. Call me back later about your schedule. The band sounds even better in person than they do on that video," she promised.

"We'll see," he responded evasively.

This time when the dead air against her ears registered, she took it as a natural progression of things. Wilson never said hello or goodbye. He was of the opinion that actions always spoke louder than any words he could possibly use.

Pushing back her chair, Whitney rose from the small desk. She was mildly surprised that exhaustion hadn't caught up with her yet. After all, she hadn't slept except to rest her eyes a couple of times during the night when she'd put her head down on the desk. However she'd hardly closed her eyes for more than a few minutes at a time and no self-respecting feline would even allow what she'd done to be called a catnap.

She paused for a moment, wondering if she should try to get at least an hour or so of sleep before heading out to the diner for some breakfast. After all, it wasn't as if she was exactly facing a full agenda.

For the first time in years, she was actually at loose ends. She could, of course, ask the owner of Murphy's—the *head* owner, she amended—if any other bands played at his saloon or if that was strictly Liam's spot. But after she received her answer—and she had a strong suspicion that Liam and his band were the sole occupants of that position—there was nothing left for her to actually *do*…unless, of course, her car was ready. However, she had a strong suspicion that it wouldn't be.

Now what? You always keep talking about what

you'd do if you had some downtime. Well, congratu-
lations, Whit. This is officially downtime. Now what?
the voice in her head repeated.

She had no answer. Some people, she concluded,
weren't built for inactivity—and she most definitely
was one of them.

She didn't do "nothing" well.

Walking up to the door of her suite, she pulled it
open just as Liam was about to knock on the other side.
Her forward momentum caused her to lose her balance
and all but fall into him.

To keep her from stumbling, Liam instinctively
made a grab for her. He wound up pulling her against
his hard torso.

Rather than act surprised, he merely smiled at her
and said, "Hi. I came to take you to breakfast."

She congratulated herself for not yelping like an
idiot. Instead, she had pulled herself together and
calmly said, "Sounds like a plan." Then, when Liam
continued standing where he was, his arms still very
much around her, Whitney asked, "Doesn't your plan
involve walking out of here?"

He smiled into her eyes, bringing her body tempera-
ture up by five degrees.

"It does," he answered.

Her breath was just about solidifying in her lungs.
She managed to push out a single word. "Today?"

His smile only grew wider as Liam assured her,
"Absolutely."

Keep talking, Whit. Keep talking. He can't kiss a
moving target—no matter how much you really want
him to, she upbraided herself.

"Then what seems to be the problem?" she asked him after a beat.

"No problem," he said easily, then went on to tell her honestly, "I just like the way it feels to have my arms around you so I thought—if you don't have any objections—that I'd just absorb that feeling a little bit longer."

Okay, there went her heart, she thought, going into double time. She had to get this under control, get out in front of it before she just gave in to the desires that were beginning to blossom—big-time—inside of her.

"How much is 'a little bit longer'?" she asked.

The end of her question was punctuated not just with an implied question mark, but her stomach made a gurgling sound, the kind of sound that went along with someone missing a meal—or two.

"I believe time has been called," Liam said, instantly raising his hands in an upward position, dramatically releasing her.

Just in time, she thought with relief. She'd been inches away from giving in to the overwhelming desire she had to kiss him.

Clearing her throat, she asked, "Where are we going for breakfast?"

"Same place we'd go for lunch and dinner," Liam replied. "Miss Joan's diner."

"There really is no other place to eat in town?" Because of where she came from, she was having a great deal of trouble wrapping her mind around the concept.

"Not unless someone invites you over to their home for a meal," he said.

"So Miss Joan has a monopoly," Whitney concluded. "That doesn't exactly encourage the woman to put her best foot forward and make sure the meals are fresh, satisfying and inexpensive."

"If you think that," Liam told her, "then you *really* don't know Miss Joan. That lady is always making sure her cooks use the freshest cuts, the best selections, and looking for bargains is second nature to her.

"It might just look like another greasy spoon," he continued, growing a shade more defensive of the woman who was dear to them all, "but nothing could be further from the truth. Angel Rodriguez is in charge of the kitchen and she's always trying out new recipes as well as keeping some of the older favorites on the menu.

"It's probably the closest think to home cooking my brothers and I have had in years," he said.

Whitney laughed and shook her head. "You make Miss Joan's diner sound like it's a slice of heaven."

"If heaven came in slices," he said, using her analogy, "then Miss Joan's would certainly be a top contender." They were outside now and despite the slight chill in the air, the sun was out and it promised to be a perfect day. Liam debated walking to the diner rather than taking his truck. Walking won out. "You got any plans for this morning and early afternoon?" he asked her.

Plans were something she could make once she was mobile again. Lengthening her stride, Whitney kept up with him. "That all depends on if my car's ready or not."

Liam was way ahead of her when it came to a status report on her car. He had made it a point to swing by the mechanic's corner shop on his way over to the hotel.

"I just checked with Mick," he told her as gently as

he could, sensing the news might upset her. "I think you might have to go with 'or not' for the time being."

"Then I guess I have no plans," Whitney said as they walked into the diner. "Why?"

"Good, because you have plans now," Miss Joan informed her in the same cadence a drill sergeant might use if he were trying to soften his approach to shouting out orders on a regular basis.

"Excuse me?" Whitney asked. She cocked her head as if that would make her hear better—or at least absorb what was being said better. She was certain that she couldn't have heard Miss Joan correctly. The woman wasn't ordering her around—was she?

"You'll be helping the rest of us finish decorating the tree," Miss Joan told her in no uncertain terms. "Can't have it standing there like that, half-done, now can we?"

The question was pointedly directed at her.

"Not if I can help it." Whitney meant it as a joke, saying the sentence tongue in cheek. However, judging by the look on Miss Joan's thin face, the woman seemed to accept her statement at face value.

"Glad to have you join us," Miss Joan continued, her face softening just a tad as her eyes swept over Liam and then back to the stranger in their midst.

Something akin to approval had the old woman's mouth curving in just the smallest of smiles.

Now what was all that about? Whitney couldn't help wondering. She strongly doubted that her mere presence was enough to get the owner of the diner to appear so pleased. It had to be something else.

But, looking around, she saw nothing out of the

ordinary—except that all the stools at the counter were filled and it looked as if no one had ordered anything yet.

That could only mean one thing. This had to be Miss Joan's work crew, Whitney thought. These were Miss Joan's dedicated Christmas Elves.

The label had Whitney smiling to herself.

Liam leaned over and asked in a hushed voice, "What's so funny?"

"I wouldn't know where to begin," Whitney whispered back.

"At the beginning would be my first suggestion, but anywhere you feel comfortable would be my next one. In the meantime," he continued when she didn't say anything, "why don't we order you some breakfast?"

Not waiting for her to agree, Liam raised his hand to catch the attention of any of the waitresses currently working in the diner.

Less than thirty seconds later, a dark-haired young woman with deep brown eyes was heading their way. She looked to be no older than about nineteen. "Can I get you anything?" she asked.

Liam turned toward Whitney and asked, "What would you like?"

A repeat of last night's kiss were the first words that streaked across Whitney's brain. Startled, she quickly banked them down. "How about just coffee and toast?"

Liam nodded, but when he placed the order with the waitress, it had somehow managed to expand. "The lady will have coffee, toast and an order of scrambled eggs, sausage and hash browns. And so will I," he added, flashing a smile at Whitney.

"Is someone else joining us?" Whitney asked him the moment the waitress withdrew. "Because that wasn't my order."

"No," he agreed. "But I thought you might need your strength. You can always leave whatever you don't want to eat on your plate," Liam told her, then added, "You look a little tired. Rough night?"

"No night," she answered. "That is, I didn't get any sleep. I was too busy editing the video."

"Video?" he repeated, confused. She hadn't mentioned anything like that last night when he'd dropped her off at the hotel. "What video?"

She looked at him. Hadn't he seen her taping him and his band last night? "One I took of you and the band performing at the saloon. Didn't you see me recording?" she asked in surprise.

"All I saw was you."

Now, why did a simple phrase like that suddenly send waves of heat all through her body, taking her from a nice, stable 98.6 to practically 100 plus in less time than it took to scramble those eggs that he had ordered for her breakfast?

Don't dwell on it, she commanded herself. There were no answers that way, only more questions. Questions and a whole nest of desires that could *not* be addressed at this time—if ever.

Clearing her throat, she went back to the subject under discussion. "Well, I had my smartphone in my hand and I was filming you and your band. I got a handful of your songs and then I stayed up editing and tweaking the footage until it popped."

The term seemed out of place where she used it. "It broke?" he asked her.

"No, it popped," she repeated, then realized that he *had* heard her. He just didn't understand what she meant. "That means it was perfect," she explained.

"Oh." He grinned at the compliment. "Then why didn't you say so?"

"I thought I did," Whitney countered. She had to remember that they were rather out of the loop here— or maybe she was just from a place where pretentiousness abounded, she amended. In that case, she needed to watch that and rein herself in.

A beat later, Liam lifted his shoulders in a dismissive shrug. "Guess I need to brush up my language skills. Anyway, Miss Joan said that everyone's to come and finish working on the tree today. Personally, I think it's going to take an extra day—if not two, before we're finished." He wrapped his hands around the coffee mug, absorbing its heat. "This is some monster we brought off the mountain," he quipped. "It's enough to give a guy a complex. Couldn't even finish decorating a simple little Christmas tree."

Her basic instincts had always been protective and now were no different. "It's neither little nor simple," she told him.

"When you two are finished," Miss Joan said, delivering their breakfasts to them personally, "get yourselves on down to the town square and get started." The woman began to leave, then remembered something. Turning around, she said, "Oh, by the way, your breakfasts are on me."

Liam protested and began taking out his wallet. Miss Joan's eyes narrowed.

"Keep your money, boy. I intend to take the amounts out in trade. That tree needs to be decorated," she repeated. "The sooner that's done, the sooner our holiday season kicks into gear—even if the weather doesn't want to cooperate."

With that, she disappeared into the kitchen.

Chapter Thirteen

Whitney found herself hurrying through the meal she initially hadn't even wanted. All it had taken was one bite, coupled with the tempting aroma of warm, crisp bacon, to resuscitate her appetite. She realized that she actually *was* hungry.

Even so, the reason behind her powering through the meal wasn't spurred on because of hunger but because she was far more focused on what would happen once breakfast was out of the way.

Her speedy consumption did not go unnoticed. "Any particular reason you're eating as if you just went the last forty-eight hours without any food?" Liam asked, amused as he watched her clean her plate at lightning speed.

Whitney spared him a quick glance, then went back to eating. "So Miss Joan doesn't come out and lecture me about wasting food."

"And?" he asked, waiting for her to tell him the real reason.

Whitney raised her eyes again. Okay, he'd caught her. She supposed there was no shame in admitting this.

"And I want to get back to decorating the tree,"

she confessed. When her mouth curved, he could have sworn the smile that graced her lips was on the shy side. "I forgot how much fun it could be."

He hoped that he would never get so busy that he put his personal life and family traditions on hold. Curious about the woman he'd rescued, Liam asked, "When was the last time you decorated a Christmas tree?"

Whitney paused for so long, he thought she'd decided not to answer him. And then, to his surprise, she told him. "The year before my mother…left."

She looked uncomfortable about her admission. He wondered why.

"Left," Liam repeated. "Is that a euphemism or…?"

"It's a description," she replied, doing her best to sound distant and having very little luck about it. "My mother left." Even now, so many years later, the words she was uttering felt as if they were comprised of cotton and sticking to her tongue and throat. "She took off with this guy who was a couple of years older than Wilson, my oldest brother."

Her expression was rueful as she continued. "Christmas was canceled that year. And the year after that. There didn't seem to be much point in celebrating it. My father had never been much for that kind of thing anyway—it was my mother who handled the holiday celebrations, the buying and wrapping of presents, things like that. My father was always too busy earning a living."

She sighed, struggling not to sound bitter. "I think that's why she took up with Roy in the first place. My mother was a beautiful woman—she always looked as if she'd just stepped out of a fashion magazine—

and Roy paid attention to her. He talked with her—not at her—and just like that, my mother was in heaven.

"And then my father found out about Roy and he gave her an ultimatum. It was him or Roy." Whitney paused for a moment as she struggled to gain some sort of control over herself, keeping the words she was saying from hurting her. "She picked Roy—and just like that, she was gone."

Leaning in, Liam asked her gently, "How old were you?"

"Eleven." Her meal finished, Whitney pushed the plate away and squared her shoulders. "So to answer your question, the last time I decorated a Christmas tree, I was eleven."

Finished as well, Liam rose to his feet and smiled at her. "Then let's get started. You've got a lot of time to make up for," he said. One hand lightly pressed against the lower portion of her spine, he gently guided her out of the diner.

Even with several blocks between the diner and the town square, she could hear the happy squeals of children enjoying themselves.

It warmed her heart.

The moment she approached the semi-decorated giant Scotch pine in the square, Whitney began to *feel* like a kid again.

There was something almost magical about the experience and the fact that she was sharing it with someone—with the man she quite literally owed her life to—just made it that much more meaningful, that much more special for her.

Because, once she was up close, the tree was so tall and so wide, several very tall ladders had been recruited and arranged in what amounted to a circle around the Scotch pine. The working theory was that with these ladders positioned for use, all the high places could be reached and decorated, as well.

That particular task would be handed over to the tallest residents of Forever, since their reach was higher than the average person's.

But that would come later. For now, there was an interweaving of bodies as young and old pitched in to make the tree presentable and uniquely theirs.

A lot of the town's citizens came and joined in for short periods of time, but most of them had work or classrooms they had to get to, some with passes stamped with a definite return time.

Whitney had no timetable to follow, no time when she had to return because she needed to be somewhere else. Consequently, decorating the tree, helping with myriad details that went along with the festive occasion, turned into almost an all-day affair.

Because her car was still with Mick, she had nowhere she needed to be. Wilson hadn't gotten back to her regarding his schedule, so for the time being, she was freer than she'd been in a very long time.

Free to enjoy herself in any way she saw fit.

And free to spend time with Liam, a man she found herself increasingly attracted to, despite her own firm promises to herself that she was not about to fall into the very same trap that had been her mother's downfall.

Her mother's actions had ruined the family, splintered it because she'd run off with a younger man, leaving her husband and children behind.

Liam wasn't that much younger than she was, but

she would still be ignoring her responsibility to her family—just as her mother had done.

Whitney refused to even *remotely* repeat history.

So she immersed herself in the enormous task of Christmas tree decorating, in volunteering to be everywhere, do everything, all under the sharp eye of one Miss Joan.

"GIRL, YOU'RE BEGINNING to wear *me* out," Miss Joan protested later that day. "And I'm just standing down here, watching you. Pace yourself," she ordered, shading her amber eyes as she looked up at Whitney.

The latter was currently balancing her weight on the step second from the top of the ladder, bracing her thighs against it as she tried to extend her reach.

"And for God's sakes, don't lean like that!" Miss Joan shouted. "C'mon down and Liam here will move the ladder for you so you can hang that ornament up properly."

Ordinarily, that would have been enough to get her instructions carried out. But Whitney made no attempt to come down.

"Whitney!" Miss Joan shouted when Whitney gave no indication that she had even heard her, much less would do as she was told.

The words were no sooner out of Miss Joan's mouth than the entire ladder moved because Whitney had shifted her weight. Listing, it began to fall to the side. The next fraction of a second saw Whitney suddenly free-falling.

Impact with the ground below was imminent.

"I gotcha!" Liam yelled as he rushed over to the

exact point where she was about to do a bone-jarring, possibly bone-breaking touchdown.

Miraculously, Liam managed to catch her. But as he did so, because of the angle, his knees buckled. They made abrupt contact with the ground, hitting it so hard that he felt his teeth all but rattling in his head.

It took everything he had not to drop her, but he managed to hold on to Whitney even more tightly.

Whitney heard him sucking in air, as if that would somehow shield him from the pain she knew he had to be experiencing.

The second she'd stopped falling and Liam came to a resting position, Whitney scrambled out of his arms. Her knees felt wobbly, but she wasn't the one she was worried about.

She looked at Liam with concern. Impact could have shattered his knees or a thigh bone. "Are you all right?" she cried.

He tried to smile and found that it took more effort than he normally expended.

"I think I'm probably two inches shorter now, but yeah, I'm all right." After struggling up to his feet, deliberately ignoring the hand she'd extended to him, Liam looked her over quickly. "Are you?"

Whitney shrugged away his question. "Other than feeling terminally stupid, I'm fine." And then her expression softened. "That's twice you saved me in less than a week," she pointed out. "If you hadn't caught me just then, I could have broken my back, or injured my spleen, or—"

She found she had to stop talking because he'd laid his index finger against her lips.

"The point is, you didn't. And the next time I catch you going up a ladder, I won't."

"You won't what?"

"I won't catch you," he told her. "You'll be on your own then. Why are you grinning?" he asked.

Her smile was warm and inviting. She was onto him.

"Because you talk big, but once a hero, always a hero," she told him, then quickly added, "That doesn't mean I plan to be reckless again. Hell, I didn't plan on being reckless to begin with. Things just devolved into that state. I'm sorry if I worried you," she apologized quietly, knowing he didn't want to attract attention to what he'd just done. "And thank you—again—for saving me."

He laughed shortly. Gratitude always left him wondering how to respond. "Yeah, well, don't mention it—and if you're really grateful—"

"Yes?" she asked, finding she had to coax the words out of his mouth.

"You'll decorate the lower branches," Liam said, pointing to that area on the tree.

Whitney turned to look at it. That particular level had been long since taken care of by Forever's children, mostly the ones under the age of eight.

"I think if the lower branches get one more decoration hung on them, the tree'll sink deep into the ground. That's a lot of concentrated weight all in a small radius."

"Then shift it," Miss Joan suggested. When Whitney continued to look at her, Miss Joan gave her a demonstration. She plucked a small decoration depicting a classic cartoon character getting all caught up in wrapping tape and paper, suffering the unfortunate state with a display of anger that was typical for this particular character.

Reaching up higher, where no child could manage to reach, Miss Joan hung up the ornament.

"See? Easy." Dusting off her hands, she signaled that her association with the decorations was now purely in an advisory capacity. "Now you do it," she told Whitney. Glancing at Liam, she added, "You, too, sunshine."

Liam gave her a mock-salute and began to shift every third decoration to a higher level.

IT FELT AS IF every bone in her body had gotten caught up in this tree-decorating venture. And now, with the tree finally dressed in all its decorative finery, those muscles and tendons were all issuing formal complaints.

With enthusiasm.

She was so tired that when Miss Joan's remaining helpers had retreated back to the diner for dinner, Whitney had trouble picking up her cup of freshly brewed coffee and bringing it to her lips.

Sitting there and trying to regroup, she was definitely too tired to chew. The idea of dinner had no appeal to her.

"I don't think I have *ever* felt this bone weary," she told Liam.

"Maybe it has something to do with the fact that you just spent the last eight hours climbing, stretching, lifting and practically being two places at once. That tree wouldn't have been finished today if not for you. Have you always been an overachiever?" Liam asked.

Whitney laughed at his question. "In my world, that's just being a plain old achiever."

"Wow. It's a wonder that you all don't burn out by the time you hit thirty," Liam marveled.

"Well, since I've already hit that so-called milestone, I guess I should consider that a compliment," she replied.

"Lady," he said, "everything about you suggests a compliment. You are, quite honestly, the most beautiful woman I've ever seen."

"I take it you don't get out much," she commented.

"I get out plenty," he assured her.

Whitney took out her phone and glanced at the screen.

"I didn't hear it ring," he said, assuming that was why she'd taken out the cell phone.

"That's because it didn't," she replied. "I was just checking to see if I missed a call." Closing the cover, she slipped the phone back into her pocket. "I didn't," she said with a sigh.

"You're not eating," Miss Joan accused, coming over to their table.

"Too tired to eat," Whitney told the woman.

"Well, you did a bang-up job and I owe you a steak dinner anytime you want to take me up on it," Miss Joan said. "I always pay my debts," she added with a wink.

"Ready to go?" Liam asked her.

She nodded. "More than ready."

Getting up, Whitney found that she wasn't quite as mobile as she thought. "Give me a second to get my legs in gear."

"I could carry you to the truck," Liam offered with a grin.

It sounded rather tempting, but the last thing she wanted was to be the center of attention.

"I'll take a rain check on that," she said, moving slowly toward the exit.

THE TRIP BACK to the hotel was short. Just as Liam pulled up to the entrance, Whitney's curiosity got the better of her.

"This morning, just before we left the diner, Miss Joan called you 'Sunshine.' Isn't that kind of an odd name to call a guy?" To her, it was a nickname best suited for a girl with long, flowing blond hair.

Turning the engine off, Liam shrugged. "It's a nickname she gave me years ago."

"Still doesn't explain why she calls you that," Whitney persisted.

There was no point in not answering her question. He'd stopped being embarrassed by it long ago. "It's because of my smile."

Whitney narrowed her eyes. "Your smile?"

Okay, maybe he was just a tad embarrassed about it, he decided. But he pushed on, thinking he probably had no choice in the matter. He had a feeling that Whitney would only keep after him until he gave her a satisfactory answer.

"Miss Joan claims it looks like sunshine when I'm really smiling." He shrugged. "I'd rather just drop the subject, okay?" he asked.

"Okay," Whitney agreed. It hadn't been her intention to make him uncomfortable. She'd just been curious. "But since we're talking about dropping it—"

"Yes?"

She forced herself to make eye contact even though

she felt like fidgeting inside and just staring at the truck's floor. "What I told you about my mother this morning, I'd rather just keep it between the two of us if you don't mind."

"I don't mind at all," he was quick to assure her. And then, because the moment seemed to call for it— or maybe because his guard was completely down, he said, "It seems kind of nice, keeping your secret." He paused for a moment. "It makes me feel close to you," he admitted.

"I would have thought that saving my life and my butt all in under a week's time would have done that," Whitney quipped.

"Well, it certainly didn't hurt," he agreed. Uncoupling his seat belt, Liam turned toward her and said, "Anytime you need saving, I'm your man."

Whitney immediately focused on the last part of his sentence.

I'm your man.

Ah, if only, she couldn't help thinking.

"Actually," he continued, slowly threading his fingers through her hair, "I'm your man no matter what it is that you need." Liam's voice was just barely above a whisper.

He'd been struggling with his reaction to her for the better part of the evening, especially during this short—and intimate—drive to the hotel.

Now, breathing in her perfume, sitting mere inches away from her, Liam couldn't think of anything else *but* her.

"I'll keep that in mind," she told him, her heart going into overdrive as she suddenly felt the space in the truck's cab shrink.

"You do that," Liam replied, his eyes caressing her face.

The next moment, he couldn't hold himself in restraint any longer. Leaning forward, he brought his mouth down on hers.

Unlike the other two times he had kissed her, this time the merest hint of contact shook his world. She'd unleashed a huge need in him, a void that for some unknown reason he felt only *she* could fill. She, with her unique way of dealing with life, with her almost childlike joy when it came to something so simple as decorating a Christmas tree, albeit a hugely oversize one.

Liam had always been lucky when it came to women. He'd had his share of women to make love with. But as much as he always got along with them and retained their friendship long after the fact, none of them had ever fired up his imagination and his soul the way that this one did.

Sitting beside her like this and not having her was sheer torture. He hadn't realized just how much torture until this very moment.

THIS WAS WRONG.

It went against everything she had said that she didn't want. Everything she'd promised herself she wouldn't do because that would mean following in her mother's footsteps.

Granted there were no husband and children gathered together in the wings, waiting to be abandoned, but the similarity between the two scenarios was impossible to miss. Her mother had run off with a younger man. Liam was younger than she was. She'd looked him up—public records were incredibly easy to access if a person knew what they were doing, and she did. She'd been right. He was close to being almost four years younger than she was. While the span wasn't nearly as much as the one that had existed between her mother and Roy, it was still there, ready to haunt her if she took any more of a misstep.

And yet—

And yet, she just couldn't find it in her heart to resist, to turn him away. Couldn't force herself to get out of the truck and just walk into the hotel, leaving him behind her.

She knew him well enough now to be confident that he wouldn't follow her if she didn't want him to.

The trouble was she did.

Chapter Fourteen

"You're thinking too hard," Liam told her just before he leaned in and kissed first one side of her mouth, then the other. "I can practically see the steam coming out of your ears," he teased softly, brushing his lips across hers lightly.

Even before he began to kiss her, Whitney was melting. It wasn't just her body, but all her pep talks to herself that were dissolving right along with her.

"That steam has nothing to do with thinking," she whispered back.

"Oh?"

There was way too much innocence infused into that single word. She knew that *he* knew exactly what he was doing to her.

Even so, Whitney could feel herself responding that much more.

Wanting him that much more.

"Yes, 'oh,'" she said, doing her best to sound distant, or at least neutral. But she was failing miserably and she knew it.

The only thing that could save her—from her own desires, let alone his—was actual distance. She needed to put real distance between them.

"I'd better go in," Whitney announced in a shaky voice.

Liam nodded, understanding. He wasn't about to push what was clearly going on between them if she was the least bit uncomfortable about it. He'd just go home and take a shower. *An extra long, really cold shower,* he told himself. Maybe one that lasted an hour...or two.

Getting out of his truck, Liam came around to her side and opened the door for her. Whitney swung her legs out, went to stand, and her knees seemed to have liquefied.

The second she began to sink, she made a grab for Liam to keep herself from hitting the ground.

He was even quicker than she was. Steadying her, he closed his arms around her tightly.

"Are you all right?" he asked, his eyes sweeping over her, taking their own inventory.

Saying yes seemed ludicrous, given what had just happened, so she said, "Just a little wobbly." Whitney looked at him, embarrassed. "Just give me a minute to get my land legs back," she said, doing her best to make a joke out of the situation.

"I've got a better idea," Liam said. The next moment, he scooped her up into his arms and began to walk to the hotel's entrance.

Caught off guard, Whitney cried, "What are you doing?"

He merely smiled at her as he shouldered open the entrance door. Moonlight streaming in through the surrounding glass illuminated the lobby as he carried her to her first-floor suite.

"I'm implementing my better idea," Liam answered easily.

"I *can* walk," Whitney protested. When he gave her a very dubious look, she amended her initial statement. "Eventually. It'll just take me a minute—or two," she murmured, thinking of her last experience.

One shoulder raised and lowered in a careless, dismissive shrug. "This saves time," he said.

She knew that Liam was just trying to be helpful, but unfortunately he was *way* too close to her. It was hard enough resisting the man when he was clear across the length of a room. Right now, she was close enough to him to breathe in the breath he exhaled.

In addition, being so close to Liam wreaked havoc on her resolve, on all her resolutions to just view him the way she did any other performer she'd signed for the family recording label.

Being close to Liam made her acutely aware of how drawn to the man she was.

Anticipation began to surface, taking her prisoner. Desire and passion suddenly became united, making demands, causing her willpower to sizzle away in the heat that was swiftly taking firm control of every inch of her body.

Whitney wasn't altogether sure just when she had laced her arms around the back of his neck. All she was truly aware of was that when he reached her suite and brought her inside, she didn't want to be here alone. Didn't want him to go.

Still holding her in his arms, he asked, "Are you okay to stand?"

"Yes," she answered much too quickly. When he began to set her down and one of her knees buckled, she had to change the "yes" to a "no" as she grabbed on to his shoulders.

"Maybe I should just put you on the bed," he suggested, indicating with his eyes the single queen-size bed behind her.

She barely turned her head to look. Pulses in her throat and wrists throbbed. Hard.

"Okay," she murmured.

But when he gently put her down, Liam found that she had wrapped her hands around the front of his jacket. When Whitney went down, so did he.

Caught by surprise, Liam wound up on top of the woman he was trying to help.

"Looks like you're not the only one who's lost their balance," he said.

She knew what he was doing. He was trying to give her a way out as a last resort.

Whitney didn't take it.

Didn't want to take it.

What she wanted this very moment, more than anything, was to feel his mouth on hers again. Feel his passion unleashing.

Still holding the front of his jacket, she yanked hard and managed to throw him off balance again just enough to get him to cover her body with his once more.

Coming in contact with the hardening contours of his torso sent a hot thrill all through her body.

At the same time, she raised her head and captured his lips with her own.

The kiss had *surrender* written all over it. Whether that was intended for him or a message to herself wasn't really clear, but since neither of them wanted a way out any longer tonight, it really didn't matter.

All that mattered was that they were right here, right now, and there was no one to argue them out of their feelings for one another.

She knew better than to be here…with him. But the chasm between knowing and doing could be leagues long and, right now, all she wanted was for Liam to make her feel wanted.

Feeling loved would have been even better, but she wasn't a child. She knew that this wasn't happy-ever-after. That happened in fairy tales. She only wanted a little happiness that existed for a few hours.

Liam would appreciate that. After all, what man Liam's age was looking for forever, anyway? A golden evening, or stellar weekend, was the longest period of time she felt she could possibly hope for.

It was enough.

Or so she told herself. The world she came from didn't have lasting relationships. All she had to look to were her parents to know that.

THE MOMENT SHE pulled him down onto her, the second she locked her lips with his, Liam realized that he was essentially a goner. He was utterly, hopelessly intrigued by this woman. Noble instincts could only last for so long and Whitney had melted his away in the heat of her mouth as it went questing over his.

His head spinning, his lips completely occupied, Liam began to caress her body. With each pass of his hands, he became more and more possessive of her, making her his own.

Rather than shrink back, Whitney pushed herself

against his hands. The small noises that escaped her lips, the tiny catches in her breath, all urged him on to greater plateaus.

He peeled her out of her clothing, one garment at a time, one side at a time.

For every item that he pulled away from her twisting, damp body, one was dragged away from his. She became as bold as he was and it only heightened his desire for her.

Their bodies became more and more entangled with one another.

Her breath grew shorter and shorter. She just couldn't seem to get enough of him. But still, a distant image of her mother wrapped up in Roy's arms haunted her. Haunted her to the point that even now, in the middle of their communal explorations, she lifted her head and asked, each word an effort, "Are you sure that you're just twenty-seven?"

The question took him aback, but only for a moment. With his heart hammering wildly, he told her, "I'll be anything you want me to be, any age. Whatever makes you happy." Framing her face with his hands, he looked into her eyes and whispered, "It's just a number, nothing else."

Then, to make his case and to get her mind off something that should have had absolutely no bearing on what they were feeling at this moment, Liam began to stroke her body, *really* stroke it, his lips softly trailing in the wake of his fingers, kissing every part of her that he had just touched.

He could tell by the way her breathing became more labored, more shallow, that he had succeeded in stirring her up even further.

Liam caressed and made love to each and every part of her for as long as he could hold himself in check. He brought her to her first climax by deftly using both his mouth and his fingers to stimulate her and bring her up and over to the ecstasy they both craved.

Her pleasure only intensified his own.

IT WAS AT THAT moment that Whitney realized that while she'd had sex before, she had never experienced lovemaking until just now. What her body was going through—what *she* was going through—felt so very different from those other times.

It felt so different that had anyone asked her to describe what was happening to her, she would have been hard-pressed to find the words to properly—or even improperly—describe it.

The closest she could come was to say that fireworks were going off inside, the kind that created rainbows and light shows in the sky.

The kind that had her holding on to him for dear life, wanting more, afraid of having it all end.

Did anyone die of ecstasy?

It was, she discovered, exquisite agony—and she was gripping it as hard as she could, by just her fingertips.

Liam finally drew the length of his body up along hers. She wiggled beneath him in heightened anticipation. With his eyes locked on hers, Liam balanced his weight between his elbows, and then he entered her.

The second he did, her breathing became more audible, her body tensed for a split second, then instantly became more fluid. Her mouth curved beneath his. A surge of excitement coursed through her veins.

Liam began to move his hips.

Whitney mimicked every move, grasping his shoulders so hard it was almost as if letting go would suddenly cause her to slip away from the earth's gravitational pull and she would go drifting through space.

The urgency within her made the rhythm more frantic as they both scrambled toward the peak that they knew waited to be claimed.

When they finally reached it a fraction of a moment later, a shower of euphoria rained on them, drenching them both.

"Incredible," Liam said, smiling and holding on to the feeling, holding on to *her*, for as long as he possibly could.

"Incredible," she echoed.

Something within him hoped the moment would last forever.

But it didn't.

And as it slowly faded away beyond their grasp, reality was there, waiting for them, waiting as they came spiraling down to earth.

He knew the second it happened for her. Her heart abruptly ceased pounding hard in double time.

Even so, it slowly settled down to a normal beat, although that took some time.

The euphoria created in the wake of their lovemaking might have been gone, but the feelings he'd had when this had all begun were still very much with him. Feelings of protectiveness, of tenderness, still flourished within his heart.

But along with those, there was another feeling, one that was entirely new to him.

It was a feeling that he'd thought he'd experienced once or twice in his life. But even so, when he tried to examine that feeling, it would suddenly just fade away, disappearing entirely as if it had never existed at all.

But this time, as he tried to explore it, the feeling remained just where it was, as strong as it had been at its inception. Liam had a very strong feeling that this time, what he was experiencing wouldn't disappear no matter how much time he gave it.

So many sensations were slamming into him, making him want things, tugging him in all different directions at the same time. He took a breath, trying to pull himself together so he could sort things out.

Gathering her to him, he kissed the top of her head. He could feel himself wanting her all over again. "See? I told you," he said softly.

She twisted so that she could see at least part of his face, her cheek rubbing against his hard, bare chest. "Told me what?"

"That age didn't matter." And then he grinned, mischief gleaming in his eyes. "You kept up just fine, granny."

Doubling up her fist, Whitney punched his arm.

"Ouch!" he cried, pretending that her punch had actually hurt.

"Is this the part where you say love hurts?" he asked, tongue in cheek.

The word pulled her up short. "Love?" she repeated in stunned disbelief.

Was he implying that he thought she loved him—or was he saying that he was entertaining stronger emotions than those made of wet tissues? Either way, she knew she couldn't ask him. That would put both of them on the spot no matter which answer he gave.

Most likely, he'd lie to hide the truth—or tell her the truth and hide it amid a joke.

One way or the other, she wasn't going to get to the truth of the situation tonight. Quite possibly never.

The only path opened to her was to just brazen it out.

"Who said anything about love?" she asked as flippantly and nonchalantly as she could.

"Well, since the voice was rather deep, I'm guessing it was me," he said, doing his best to keep a straight face. "Gonna hold it against me?" he asked.

"No, of course not," she said quickly. The last thing she wanted was for him to say anything he didn't want to say.

How had this gotten so complicated so quickly?

"You just said it in the heat of the moment," she reasoned.

"It wasn't the moment that was hot," he replied, his eyes slowly assessing the length of her. All that accomplished was to make himself crazy all over again, Liam thought. "It was me—and it was you. And if I get a vote in this, I was kind of hoping you would hold it against me—right along with that delicious body of yours," he said.

Whitney was certain that she wasn't understanding him correctly. Her brain felt muddled and all she could really think of was making love with him again—she had to be losing her mind.

Where the hell was her sense of self-preservation? she silently demanded.

She shook her head as if to try to clear it, even though she knew that wouldn't accomplish anything. "What?"

"Guess I'm not making myself clear. Looks like I'm just going to have to show you," he said out loud. "I'm better at showing than telling, anyway," he told her just before he went on to demonstrate just what he meant by sealing his mouth to hers.

Whitney slipped willingly back into the land of ecstasy—right alongside of the man who took her there.

Chapter Fifteen

The rhythmic buzzing noise wouldn't stop.

It wormed its insistent way into Whitney's consciousness like a malcontented intruder, ultimately dissolving her sleep.

Reluctantly, after several tries, Whitney finally managed to pry her eyes open. Only when she finally succeeded did she realize that she'd fallen asleep. The next moment, she became aware of the fact that she hadn't fallen asleep alone.

Bolting upright, her heart racing, she found herself looking down into Liam's peaceful face. He was still asleep—or at least it looked that way to her.

However, the next moment, with his eyes still closed, she heard Liam ask, "Aren't you going to get that? I think it's your cell phone. I turned mine off last night."

Disoriented, Whitney scanned the room, trying to home in on where the sound was coming from so she could find her phone.

"It's okay, you can get up," he murmured, barely opening his eyes so that they formed slits. "I won't peek if that's what you're afraid of."

"It's a little late for that," she murmured under her

breath. He was right, though. She couldn't spot her phone if she stayed in bed. Whitney got up.

"Glad you feel that way," he responded, opening his eyes all the way. He made no attempt to pretend that he wasn't looking at her. Seeing her like that stirred him all over again. "You're just as beautiful in the morning light as you looked last night," he told Whitney.

The compliment both pleased her and upset her at the same time. She loved making love with Liam but even so, she was annoyed with herself for not having enough inner strength to resist him.

Playing a hunch, Liam leaned over the side of the bed and looked under it. The phone was there, having somehow been kicked under her bed during the initial frenzy last night. Retrieving it now, Liam held the phone out to her.

It was still buzzing.

"Better answer it before they hang up," he advised. His eyes washed over her possessively. "Sounds important."

Whitney flushed, embarrassed, as she took the phone from him. "Hello?"

"You sure took your sweet time answering." The deep, critical voice was unmistakable. Wilson. "Where were you?"

Talk about bad timing, she thought. Leave it up to her older brother to interrupt things. The only way it would have been any worse was if he had called her while she and Liam were in the middle of making love. She supposed she should be grateful for smaller favors.

"Sorry, I was in the shower," she apologized, saying the first thing that popped into her head. Out of the corner of her eye, she saw Liam's amused expression. She turned her head away.

"Well, dry yourself off and get ready to pick me up at the airport," Wilson informed her. He rattled off the airline and flight number. "It's supposed to be landing in an hour, but you know how reliable *that* is. I'm just hoping to get there before evening—it'll mess up my return time," he told her before she could ask.

She braced herself for her brother's disapproval. "I can't pick you up, Will. My car's being repaired, re-member?"

She could almost *see* the frown burning itself into his face. She certainly heard it in his voice when she asked, "And there're no other cars in this town?"

"None that are mine," she answered. "I could see if I might be able to rent someone's truck for a couple of hours," she offered.

"A truck?" Wilson echoed in clear disdain. He sounded as if she'd just suggested he gather several pigs together and wallop in the mud with them. "Never mind, I'll rent a car at the airport."

"Do you want directions on how to get here?" she asked, struggling to come across as helpful.

In actuality, she was finding it increasingly more difficult to think straight because Liam was tracing patterns with his fingertips along her bare spine, then following his tracings with a light trail of kisses, none of which was conducive to coherent thought.

"Thanks, but if my GPS can't locate your hick town, I'm turning around and booking a flight home imme-diately," Wilson told her.

And then he was gone.

With a sigh, Whitney put her phone on the night-stand.

"He upset you," Liam noted, turning her so that she partially faced him.

She pulled the sheet up around herself. "He's my brother. He thinks that's his job." And then she forced herself to brighten. "But the good news is that the video I sent him of you and the band impressed him enough for Will to come out here to see you perform in person."

She just wished her brother had given her a heads-up about *when* he was coming here instead of just turning up, so she could have been more prepared.

"If you and the band play even half as well as you did the other night, I think you can consider yourselves on your way to fame and fortune." She grinned at Liam. "You'll get the life you've always wanted."

"Well, if that *does* happen, then you're the lady who *made* it happen," he said.

Then, just like that, he pulled her into his arms and kissed her soundly, putting his heart into it.

Whitney knew she should be getting both herself—and Liam—ready, but all she could think of was making love with him again. When she was with him, she completely forgot to be logical.

"Liam," she breathed, her head spinning. "You have to stop that. I can't think when you do that."

"Funny, me, neither," he admitted just before he kissed her again.

After that, everything else was put on temporary hold.

WILSON MARLOWE'S DARK BROWN eyes missed nothing. He looked slowly around Murphy's. His reaction was not particularly difficult to gauge in view of the disdainful expression on his rather thin face.

Murphy's was not up to his standards. It had been a long time since he had haunted places like this, looking for unnoticed talent.

"I flew all the way from LA for this?" he asked his sister.

"No, you flew all the way from Los Angeles to see the band perform in person," she reminded him. "'This' is just where they play. Besides, I think this place is quaint. It grows on you."

"Maybe on you, but I have standards," Wilson informed her dismissively. A sound that was close to a laugh escaped his lips. "I guess this means I won't be involved in a bidding war to get them to sign a contract with Purely Platinum. I'm still undecided about signing them at all," Wilson was quick to add when he saw the hopeful expression cross Whitney's face.

Wilson's flight had been delayed a number of hours and when he finally arrived in Forever, he was in less than good spirits.

"Well, I hope this trip convinces you of their talent," she said. The moment he crossed the threshold to the saloon, Whitney could feel her whole body instantly grow tense. She wanted this break for Liam and his band in the worst way. She was going on instincts, something she had honed over the past ten years, and she believed in Liam and the Forever Band. The band—especially Liam—was talented and had a great deal of potential.

But Wilson was the type who allowed more than just appreciation of good performers guide the decisions he ultimately made. There were times when she had

seen him pass on a performer because he had taken a
basic dislike to them for no apparent reason. In general, Wilson was good, but he was not above pettiness.

"Do all these other people have to be here?" he
asked Whitney, waving his hand around the room to
generally include all the other patrons.

"Will, they're paying customers here. I can't ask
Brett to clear the place so that the acoustics are better,"
she protested. "Besides, don't you want to see how the
performers interact with their audience?"

"Audience," he repeated, as if exploring the term.
"Don't you mean the people who they've known all
their lives?" His contempt was obvious. "Not particularly. They like them," he observed, listening to the wel-
coming applause just before the band played their first
number. "Big surprise," he snorted.

He was going to be difficult about this, Whitney
thought. And yet, he'd come all this way, so he had to
believe it was worth the effort. Her brother never did
anything just to be accommodating.

"Wilson, why don't you try just listening and putting
your cynicism on hold for a change?" she suggested.

Wilson merely shrugged in response. But at least he
remained where he was rather than stalking out. With
Wilson, anything was possible. Having him here was
a small victory in itself.

Whitney mentally crossed her fingers and smiled
her encouragement to Liam and the rest of the band as
they began to play.

DURING THE NEXT forty-five minutes, Whitney slanted
a glance toward her brother several times, trying to
gauge whether or not Wilson liked what he was hear-

ing. On the one hand, she couldn't see how he couldn't, but on the other, he was Wilson and Wilson had always behaved unpredictably.

She honestly believed that her brother took a certain amount of satisfaction in being that way.

Finally, the last number was over and the band took a short break. During that entire set, Wilson hadn't said a single word and she just couldn't stand not knowing any longer.

"Well?" she asked eagerly. "What do you think of them?"

Wilson inclined his perfectly styled head slightly, as if considering her question for the very first time. "Good," he finally pronounced. "Needs work," he emphasized, then continued in a loftier tone, "but good." Looking at her, he asked, "When can he fly to LA?" he asked.

She felt elated and released the breath she'd been holding. Her brother liked the band!

"Well, you'd have to ask— Wait," she said, suddenly focusing on the exact words her brother had just used. "You just said 'he.'"

"Yes," he said coolly. "I know. Your point?"

He couldn't be saying what she thought he was saying. "Don't you mean when can the band fly out?"

His tone bordered on exasperated annoyance. "If I had meant the 'band,' I would have *said* the 'band.' Or, in a pinch, 'they.'" His eyes narrowed as he looked at her. "But I didn't, did I?"

No, he hadn't, she thought, getting a sinking feeling in the pit of her stomach. This wasn't going to go over well with Liam. The band meant a great deal to him.

He'd told her that the other men who made up the band had been his friends since first grade, or thereabouts.

"You only want Liam?" Whitney asked in a stilted voice.

"If that's his name, yes, I just want him," Wilson confirmed.

"Why don't you want the whole band?" Whitney challenged.

She knew in her heart that Liam would not go for this latest twist. Yes, he wanted to succeed, but he wanted the *band* to succeed, not just him.

That was one of the reasons she'd felt so drawn to him, because he was so very loyal. That was a rare emotion in her world, where artists sold out their own mothers for a decent review.

"Because there's nothing exceptional about them," Wilson replied, sounding as if the topic bored him. "This Liam guy, however, I think he can be marketed well. He has that whole chiseled, movie-star look going on for him, plus he's got a damn good voice."

"Yes, he does," she agreed with Wilson. "But he's not going to go for it—for breaking up the band," she warned her brother.

"Then it'll be his loss," Wilson predicted, sounding unmoved. "I'm not about to deal with some self-absorbed prima donna to start with."

"That's not being a prima donna," she said fiercely. "That's being loyal. You remember loyalty, don't you, Will? It's one of those admirable traits we shed like a second skin if it gets in our way. And by 'our,' I mean 'your,'" she emphasized.

Wilson remained unmoved and unaffected. "Potato, po*ta*to, it's all one and the same to me," he told her.

Just then, Liam reached their table. He was fairly radiating sheer energy, the way he always did after delivering what he considered to be a good performance.

"Well?" he asked, allowing his eagerness to break through, glancing from Whitney to her brother. "What did you think?" he asked the latter. After all, that was why he had come, Whitney had told him.

"I think you've got a big future ahead of you, kid," Wilson said, slipping into his public persona, which for the most part, was far less dour than the Wilson he allowed his siblings to see. "Big future," he repeated with emphasis.

"Oh, wow." Liam felt as if clouds had just been substituted for solid ground beneath his feet. To want something for so long and then to be within touching distance of it, Liam found it difficult to contain himself. "Wait'll the guys hear this. Sam kept saying that we'd never make it—"

Wilson made no apologies for cutting in. "He was right."

Liam looked at Whitney's brother in confusion. He hadn't liked the man all that much when he'd first met him today, but nowhere was it written that you had to like the man who "discovered" you. He made up for it by really liking Whitney. A lot.

Still, he wanted to get this straightened out if he could. "But you just said—"

"Will said that you're the one with potential, not the band," she clarified, her voice somber.

Liam gazed at her for a long moment, sheer confusion becoming very apparent on his face. "But we're a band," he protested.

"They're just so much background," Wilson corrected him. "You're the one with star potential. I thought we'd sign you, find the right kind of songs for you, find your brand so to speak. I know a couple of background musicians I can have come in to the studio to play with you, explore your sound."

"Wait. Wait, wait," Liam said, holding up his hand. This was going much too fast and he wanted to clear it all up before he found himself agreeing to something he had no intentions of agreeing with. "Are you really telling me that you don't want the band?"

Wilson shrugged. "They're okay, kid, but you're the one with star power—given the right material and guidance," Wilson qualified pointedly. "What do you say?"

Liam glanced at Whitney before giving her brother his answer. "I say that the band and I are a set—"

"Kid, take it from me, they'll just hold you back," Wilson interrupted. And then he counseled, "Think about it for a couple of days, then give me a call."

Going into his vest pocket, Wilson retrieved a business card. He pressed it into Liam's hand. "But I'm telling you now, this is a once in a lifetime deal and if I were you I'd jump to take it."

Liam looked at the business card, then at Whitney. "What do you say?"

She could feel Wilson watching her, willing her to go along with his decision. She knew there was no way around it.

"I say that I like you *and* the band, but it's not my call. Wilson has the final word on that." *For better or for worse,* she couldn't help thinking.

Then, Wilson did what he seldom did, he coaxed. "Don't be a fool, kid. Don't turn down the opportunity of a lifetime just because you think you owe those other guys something. Take my word for it, if the tables were turned, I guarantee that they'd jump at this opportunity and leave you behind in the dust. Loyalty isn't what it's cracked up to be," Wilson concluded. He looked at his watch. "I've got to be getting to the airport. My flight back is in a couple of hours."

Whitney looked at him in surprise. "You're not even staying the night?" It seemed as if he had put in an awful lot of miles for possibly nothing.

"What for?" Wilson was asking. "I came, I heard, I pitched a contract. That was what you wanted, right? Congratulations, you were right," he allowed. "The guy's good."

"I said the *band* was good," she corrected him.

"Then maybe there shouldn't be that much more congratulating," he said. "Either way, I'll sign pretty boy over there to a contract as long as I can get him into a studio in Los Angeles. There're big things ahead of him," he promised—and Wilson, she was the first to admit, was seldom wrong. "See you back in Los Angeles," he said.

He got up and walked out before she could speak further.

"That didn't exactly go the way I'd planned," she told Liam by way of an apology as she crossed over to him. "But he did like you," she was quick to point out.

"Doesn't matter," Liam said, shrugging off her comment. "There's no way that I'm going to break up the band, to walk out on guys I've known—and practiced with—ever since I was in elementary school with them."

She wanted him to carefully consider all his options

and not just dismiss the offer because he was angry that Wilson wasn't keen on the other members of the band.

"Liam, my brother really does have the kind of connections that will open doors and could easily make your career for you."

"I can't believe I'm saying this," he said quite honestly, "but there're some things that are more important than a career. If I jumped at this, leaving Sam and Christian and Tom behind, I wouldn't be able to look at myself in the mirror every morning."

"Liam, *think* of what you're turning down," Whitney pleaded.

"I am," he told her solemnly, his eyes on hers. He assumed that she was including herself in that package deal. If he said no to her brother, if he remained here, then it was over. That stellar experience he'd just had with her last night, that was over with, as well.

"Hey, there you are," Mick called out, striding toward Whitney. "Don't mean to interrupt you two, but I knew how anxious you were to get your car back, little lady, and I just wanted to let you know that it's all done. You can come by the shop anytime and we'll settle up. She's all yours and eager to go," Mick said with a laugh.

"I guess there's nothing keeping you here, then," Liam concluded, giving her a look that all but pulled her heart out of her chest. And then he nodded toward the band. "I've got to be getting back to the guys. It's time for the next set."

With that, he turned away from her and walked back to the band.

And managed to walk over her heart in the process.

Chapter Sixteen

She was gone.

Liam moved slowly through the hotel suite. There was absolutely no trace of her. No indication that she had ever been there.

Nothing.

He wasn't sure why he'd thought that he'd still find Whitney here, in the suite where his life had suddenly changed forever. Maybe it was because neither one of them had said the word *goodbye*.

Or maybe it was because the whole last scenario between them had seemed so surreal. In what world did the woman who turned out to be the answer to his prayers also have the ability to make his professional dreams come true?

It was more of a fantasy than reality.

In any case, part of him felt that a short time-out had been in order. But that had come and gone now. A full twenty-four hours had evaporated since everything had gone sour between Whitney and him.

He wanted a mulligan or whatever the current term was for what amounted to a do-over.

He *needed* a do-over.

Liam continued to move around the suite, searching

for some small item Whitney might have forgotten to pack, but there wasn't any. Nothing he could touch or hold in his hand.

Maybe he was going crazy, but he could detect just the faintest trace of the perfume she'd worn.

He stood very still for a moment, inhaling as deeply as he could. But all he succeeded in doing was somehow neutralizing that scent.

It was gone.

As was she.

He had to face it. Whitney was gone and so was his opportunity to apologize, to tell her that whether or not his career took off didn't matter to him—the only thing that mattered was her.

Feeling incredibly empty, he slowly closed the door to the hotel suite and went back to Murphy's. Work was waiting for him.

"GREAT JOB."

Wilson's words echoed in her head as Whitney recalled the satisfied expression on her brother's face when she'd brought him the Laredo band's signed contract. She had lived up to her promise, done what she had initially set out to do. She had auditioned the pop group—the drummer had bounced back faster than anyone had hoped and had attended, propped up in his chair. They'd turned out to be as good as their demo so she had signed them to a contract. Each side felt as if they had come out ahead. It was a mutually beneficial contract.

After delivering the contract to her brother, she'd thrown herself back into traveling and making the rounds at the various clubs where, on occasion, decent new talent could be found.

"Why don't you take some time off?" Wilson had suggested the next time she'd touched base with him. "You certainly have earned it—and by my reckoning, you haven't taken any time off in years."

"I want to work," she'd answered, summarily rejecting her brother's suggestion.

What was implied, but not said, was that she *needed* to work, needed to keep moving so that she could stay ahead of her thoughts, which were still far too melancholy for her to handle.

"Well, then, by all means, work," Wilson had told her, leaning back in his swivel chair. "I'm sure as hell not going to stand in your way because—and if you tell anyone, I'll deny it—you've become even better at spotting talent than I am."

She'd looked at him then, surprised. This was definitely out of character for her brother. If she didn't know any better, she would have checked his garage for a pod to see if he'd been cloned.

"You don't have to treat me with kid gloves, Will," she'd said.

"No kid gloves," he'd immediately denied, holding up his hands as if she had the right to inspect them. "Just respect. It's about time I gave you your due." Leaning over his desk, he'd handed her the newest list of possible up-and-comers she could go check out in person before she made any arrangements for future auditions. "That should keep you busy."

Whitney had tucked the list away in her pocket without even looking at it, only saying, "Good," before she'd left her brother's office.

Though she worked frantically, she still couldn't shake the feeling that she was sleepwalking through her life.

And she ached inside.

"HAVE YOU TRIED getting in touch with her?" Brett asked out of the blue two days before Finn's wedding.

He'd been watching Liam sitting on a bar stool, just staring off into space for the past twenty minutes. He'd voiced his concern for his youngest brother, concern over the fact that in the past two weeks, Liam had moved around like a man in a trance.

Liam went through the motions of being alive, tended bar, played with his band, but it was as if his very soul had gone missing. There was nothing about Liam that even remotely hinted at the man he'd been just a short while ago.

"Liam?" Brett said, raising his voice when he received no answer. "Earth to Liam."

The third time was the charm. Hearing his brother for the first time, Liam turned toward him and said, "Yeah?"

"Have you tried getting in touch with her?" Brett repeated.

Liam glanced away. "Who?" he asked innocently.

"The Tooth Fairy," Brett retorted. "Who do you think, lunkhead? That woman you saved from drowning. The one who's got your insides all tied up in knots."

"Nobody's got me tied up in knots," Liam denied angrily.

Brett frowned, shaking his head. "You could have fooled me."

"Apparently that's not hard to do," Liam answered listlessly.

Brett tossed aside the cloth he'd been using to polish the counter. "You want me to track her down?"

For the first time in two weeks, Liam came to life. His head whipped around as he faced his older brother and all but shouted, "Hell no!"

"All right," Brett agreed. His eyes narrowed as he pinned his younger brother in place. "Then you do it."

Liam raised and lowered his shoulders in a hapless shrug.

"Nothing to do," Liam told his brother.

"Look, you've been moping around for the last two weeks and frankly, we're all worried about you."

Liam deftly turned the tables around. "And I'm worried about you because if you have nothing better to do than sit around watching me, you're in a really bad way, Brett. What's the matter? Honeymoon over for you and Lady Doc?"

"Liam—" he began.

"Drop it, Brett," Liam warned his brother. "I mean it."

"Okay, then I've got a question for you. Are you going to be able to play at Finn's wedding or should I see if I can find someone else at this late date?"

Just because he was trying to function without a heart didn't mean he couldn't do right by Finn.

"Don't worry about it. The band and I have got this," he said, his tone of voice warning his brother to back off if the latter knew what was good for not just him but for everyone.

"I hope so," Brett said evenly. "Finn wants to give Connie the wedding of her dreams and that doesn't include a hangdog front man for the band." He looked pointedly at Liam.

"As I remember, the wedding of Connie's dreams involved getting married on Christmas Day and having newly fallen snow on the ground for their wedding pictures. That sure isn't going to happen, not down here."

"That's what I mean," Brett interjected. "He's already working with a slight handicap." Brett came across as relatively easygoing, but his hackles went up when it came to anything having to do with his brothers. "I don't want you to be another one."

"No problem," Liam assured him.

"You're going to be able to play even though it's in the town square?"

"Yeah, sure." Liam shrugged dismissively.

But Brett obviously didn't consider the matter settled yet. "Even though, ever since Whitney left, you've gone out of your way *not* to walk through the town square, specifically, not to walk by the Christmas tree?" Brett looked at him knowingly.

"What are you, following me now?" Liam demanded, stunned.

"Kid, this is Forever. *Nobody's* got secrets here no matter how hard they try." He didn't need to follow Liam to get his answers. If nothing else, Miss Joan was his conduit. He could always rely on the woman to clue him into things. "Now, one last time," Brett pressed the matter for Finn's sake. "Playing in the town square, with that tree *she* helped decorate in the background, that's not going to be a problem for you?"

"The only thing that's a problem for me right now is a nosy brother who doesn't know when to back off and stop asking so many insulting questions."

Brett slowly nodded. He'd developed a very tough skin years ago when he'd had to take over running Murphy's as well as raising his two younger, orphaned brothers. A thin-skinned person would have never been able to survive, coping with everything the way that he had.

Raising his hands up halfway, Brett declared, "This is me, officially backing off."

Liam merely grunted in acknowledgment as he left the saloon. He was late for rehearsal.

IT WAS THE NOISE that woke him. The sound of large trucks drawing closer.

Liam hadn't really been able to sleep very much the past few nights. Someone would have thought it was *his* wedding today instead of Finn's by the way that he acted and felt.

Right now, it felt as if *he* was mounted on pins and needles.

Maybe it was because, in preparing for Finn's wedding and rehearsing the songs that he and the band would play, it just brought home the fact that he was never going to get married.

Up until almost a month ago, that wouldn't have even earned a blink from him. But now, it just made him realize that he would face the rest of his life alone. That there would never be someone for him the way there was for Brett and Finn.

Lightning didn't strike twice in the same place. And he had already had lightning in his life.

The noise grew louder.

It almost sounded as if it was coming from more

than one direction. What the hell was going on? he wondered, the fog around his brain lifting.

Liam headed toward the window and looked out to see what there was to see. The window faced the square and he had been avoiding looking out at or even coming near it, but now his curiosity prompted him to push back the drapes and, Christmas tree or no Christmas tree, to look out.

He supposed even the intent to do that was a good sign in his case. Maybe it meant that he was taking back his life—or maybe it meant that he was just more curious than he'd thought.

Pushing the drapes back as far as he could, Liam found himself looking at what seemed like a fleet of huge trucks. Dump trucks from their appearance. And they were dumping their contents right in the middle of the town square.

There were several white mounds in the middle of the square and they grew with each truck's deposit.

Liam blinked. Was that—

"Damn, it looks like snow!" Finn cried out, crowded in behind him.

Determined to go the traditional route, Finn had opted to spend his last night as a single male in the house where he had grown up instead of with Connie.

"You see it, too, huh?" Liam asked, staring at the white mounds.

"Damn straight I do," Finn answered excitedly. "Connie is going to *love* this." He suddenly looked at his brother. "Did you do this?"

"Me?" Not that he wouldn't have loved to take credit for this, but there was no way he could begin to pull off something like this. He hadn't a clue where this—

and the trucks that brought it—had all come from. "Where would I get snow?" Liam asked. "I can create songs. Snow's another matter entirely. Maybe Brett had it shipped," he guessed.

"From where?" Finn asked.

Damned if he knew, Liam thought. "Good point. Maybe Connie did it," was Liam's next guess.

It was a guess that Finn quickly shot down. "Connie wouldn't waste money like that. Now that she's heading her own construction company and donating all her free time to renovating the homes on the reservation, she wouldn't do something like this just to satisfy an old fantasy she had."

Finn was probably right, Liam thought. But that still didn't solve the mystery. "Well the snow didn't just drive itself here," Liam said, trying to get to the bottom of the mystery and going over to his brother's side.

Finn had been staring out the window the entire time that the dump trucks had been unloading their cargo in the square.

Looking for anything that might answer his mounting questions, Liam suddenly homed in on the person who appeared to be signing something for each driver.

A bill?

Who in their right minds would have brought in this much snow, or ice, or whatever the substance actually turned out to be? The person signing for the "cargo" turned around and Liam could make out the person's face clearly.

Son of a gun.

Finn looked rather smug. "I believe you know the lady, right?"

Liam's jaw slackened. He stood there a moment longer, as if not trusting his own eyes. He'd already made up his mind that right after Finn's wedding, he was going to move heaven and earth to find Whitney. Was this his mind just playing tricks on him?

The next moment, still only wearing his jeans and forgetting to pick up a shirt, Liam ran barefoot out of the house. He had to see if it was really Whitney.

"I guess 'right,'" Finn murmured, then announced happily to the air at large, "I've got a wedding to get ready for." He hurried off to get started.

THE GROUND WAS hard and rough on his bare feet, but Liam hardly noticed. Every fiber of his being was focused on only one thing. The woman in the center of the truck caravan.

She was back.

Unless he was having serious hallucinations, Whitney was back.

He had no intentions of losing this second chance he'd just been granted by the whimsical forces that were out there.

"Whitney!" he called out way before he was anywhere close to her.

The trucks were all rumbling and creaking, creating a veritable wall of noise all around her. Even so, she could have sworn she heard Liam calling out her name.

Most likely, it was wishful thinking on her part. Wishful thinking, too, that just because she had called in a number of favors from several ski resort managers so that she could help give Liam's future sister-in-law the wedding of her dreams, everything would be perfect between her and Liam from here on in.

She knew better than that, Whitney silently lectured herself.

At least her brain knew better. Her heart, rebel that it was, well, that was an entirely different matter. Her heart was hoping for a miracle. It was hoping for the opportunity to reconnect with Liam and, this time, to do it right.

Or at least, not to mess up too badly.

"Whitney!"

Damn it, that *was* Liam's voice. She was *certain* of it.

Whitney started to look around, doing her best to scan the immediate area. The fleet of trucks were beginning to draw a crowd on their own. People's natural curiosity had been aroused.

She could see Miss Joan approaching from the diner, saw a number of other people she recognized converging on the square as well, but Liam wasn't part of them.

Whitney could feel her heart beginning to sink a little.

Not over yet, she promised herself. *It's not over yet.*

She was prepared to do or say whatever it took to make amends with him, and—

"Damn it, woman, I'm yelling myself hoarse."

Suddenly, she felt herself being swept up as a strong pair of arms closed around her. "You came back!" she heard Liam cry one split second before he covered her mouth with his own.

After that, she was a little fuzzy about the details. All she knew was that everything became right with the world.

And this time, she intended to keep it that way.

Epilogue

It was a wedding that the people of Forever wouldn't soon forget, Miss Joan would say in the months that lay ahead. Not just because of the last-minute, unexpected appearance of snowdrifts throughout the town square to dazzle the wedding guests—snowdrifts in a town that had *never* seen any snow before. But also because, as the bride was walking down the aisle on the arm of Stewart Emerson, a man she had come to regard as her surrogate father, her own father, Calvin Carmichael, seemed to materialize out of nowhere. He quietly asked her for permission to walk her the rest of the way.

"I thought you said you couldn't get away," Connie said, totally stunned by her father's unexpected appearance.

It was one of the few times she had ever seen her father smile. "What? A man can't change his mind about seeing his only daughter get married?"

Overwhelmed, torn, she looked at Emerson, but the stately man had already gently removed her hand from his arm. Smiling encouragingly at her, Emerson nodded and fell back, allowing her father to replace him.

Connie silently blessed Emerson.

She struggled with tears the last ten feet to where the minister, and Finn, stood waiting.

By the time the ceremony was over, there was hardly a dry eye left in the crowd.

IT WASN'T UNTIL several hours later, after the professional wedding photographs had been taken and the reception had officially gotten underway, that Liam had an opportunity to actually talk with the woman who had set his life on its ear.

"Where did you get the snow?" he asked, still marveling at the winter-wonderland effect it was having on everyone, despite the fact that it had, perforce, begun to slowly melt.

Whitney was still very pleased with both herself and the way the bride had squealed in excited disbelief when she first saw the snow around the Christmas tree.

"I pulled a few strings with the managers of a couple of skiing resorts that I knew," she replied.

"That was a hell of a thing you did," Brett said, coming up to join them.

Whitney shrugged off the compliment. "A girl deserves to have the wedding of her dreams. Just so happened that I could make it come true. No big deal."

"Oh, yes," Liam contradicted, "it's a *very* big deal."

"I second the motion," Alisha, Brett's wife, said, raising her hand as if this was an actual vote being taken. Brett's arm slipped around her shoulders. Alisha flashed her husband a smile before going on to tell Whitney, "That was a really nice thing you did."

Wanting to deflect the subject away from her, Whitney asked Liam, "Do you think your band can play one song without you so we can dance?"

He was already taking her hand and leading her to the dance floor. Since he and the band were taking a break, the dance floor was presently devoid of couples.

"Consider it done," Liam said.

Looking over his shoulder toward his band members, he nodded and pointed his index and middle fingers at them. Half a beat later, the air was filled with music.

"I came back for a reason," Whitney told him as they danced.

"I know." His fingers laced through hers. They were swaying to the music. It was as if order was restored to the universe, he mused. "To bring Connie her dream wedding."

"That wasn't the only reason I came back," Whitney admitted. "Liam, I have something to tell you."

He looked at her for a long moment. "Funny, because I have something to tell you."

"Me first," she insisted. She'd been bursting with this news since she had arrived in Forever early this morning.

Liam inclined his head, humoring her. "Okay, ladies first."

It took effort not to have the words just come tumbling out over one another like so many scattered marbles. "I convinced Wilson that you needed the band—*this* band. After all, every performer has people who play backup for them, why not the people who know you like the back of their own hands? *And*—"

"There's more?" he asked in surprise.

"There's more." She beamed, excited for him. "Wilson's agreed that you should do your first music video right here in Forever. In essence, it'll put Forever on the map—so that Connie's hotel can see some decent business," she concluded. "Your turn. What did you want to tell me?"

"What I've got to say isn't going to hold a candle to what you just said," he warned her.

Whitney didn't want him to feel that way. For the first time in her life, she wasn't trying to compete, to come out on top. What she had done, she had done strictly for him. She wanted him to be happy.

"Let me be the judge of that," she coaxed, waiting to hear what he had to say.

"I was going to come out to LA next month," he said quietly.

He had succeeded in surprising her. "You decided to accept Wilson's terms for the contract?"

She would have bet money that he wouldn't change his stance on the matter. Had she been that wrong about him? Had the promise of fame seduced him, making him turn his back on loyalty?

"No," he answered emphatically. "I was going to come out to look for you." A rueful smile curved his lips. "Turns out that nobody likes me without you. They all think I've gotten surly and moody."

"You?" Whitney asked incredulously, then shook her head. "Never happen."

"Yeah, actually it did," he contradicted. "They were right. I'm not any good without you." He took a deep breath. "In case I'm not making myself clear, I love you. And even I don't like myself without you. No pressure, I just want to be around you."

"And that's all?" she asked, looking at him. "Just be 'around me'?"

He laughed shortly to himself. "Well, ideally, I'd want to marry you, but—"

"Yes!"

Liam blinked. He was too young to be losing his hearing. "Wait, what?"

"Yes," Whitney repeated, glowing.

Liam abruptly stopped dancing even though the band hadn't finished the number. "Yes?" he asked, wanting to be perfectly clear on this.

She nodded for good measure. "Yes."

He still wasn't sure they were talking about the same thing. He watched her closely as he asked, "You'll marry me?"

Her smile widened to the point that under different conditions, it might have been referred to as blinding. "Yes!"

"Hey, Liam, you're up, man!" Sam called to him, beckoning him over to the band.

"Hold on a second," he called back, his attention entirely focused on the woman who had just made him the happiest man on earth. Holding her hand, he wove his way over to the others.

"What are you doing?" Whitney asked, laughing as she trailed after him.

"You're going to sing the next number with me," he told her, tossing the words over his shoulder.

"I can't sing," she protested, tugging slightly to get her hand back. He held it fast.

"Yes, you can. I've heard you," Liam said. The next moment, he turned toward the wedding guests and addressed them. "She's going to need a little coaxing, folks. Whitney's shy, so give it up for the future Mrs. Liam Murphy."

A wave of resounding applause met the announcement. When it died down, the band began to play. Two bars into it, Whitney recognized the song. The song was all about giving your heart to the one you love.

She had no choice but to sing with Liam. Their voices blended beautifully. Just as their lives would, she couldn't help thinking.

And when the number was over, Liam surprised her again by kissing her in front of everyone.

She had no choice but to kiss him back.

It was the first time in her life that she enjoyed not having a choice.

* * * * *

Don't miss Marie's 250th romance,
CARRYING HIS SECRET,
available February 2015
from Harlequin Romantic Suspense!

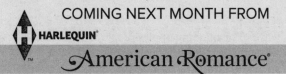

COMING NEXT MONTH FROM

H HARLEQUIN®

ℳ American Romance®

Available January 6, 2015

#1529 A COWBOY OF HER OWN
The Cash Brothers • by Marin Thomas
Porter Cash has always been commitment shy—then he has a run-in with Wendy Chin, who makes the cowboy think about settling down. But her family obligations mean Porter is the *last* man Wendy can be with!

#1530 THE NEW COWBOY
Hitting Rocks Cowboys • by Rebecca Winters
Former navy SEAL Zane Lawson has come to the ranch land of Montana to find his peace. But he won't rest until he discovers Avery Bannock's secret—the one thing keeping them from being together.

#1531 TEXAS MOM
by Roz Denny Fox
Delaney Blair swore she was through with Dario Sanchez when he left her. But for the sake of her sick child, she goes to Argentina to tell Dario that he is needed by the son he never knew he had—and by Delaney!

#1532 MONTANA VET
Prosperity, Montana • by Ann Roth
In a stroke of luck, veterinarian Seth Pettit walked into Emily Miles's shelter at a critical time. But as the charming vet becomes indispensable, Emily wonders when her luck will run out...

HARCNM1214

REQUEST YOUR FREE BOOKS!
2 FREE NOVELS PLUS 2 FREE GIFTS!

HARLEQUIN
American ★ Romance
LOVE, HOME & HAPPINESS

YES! Please send me 2 FREE Harlequin® American Romance® novels and my 2 FREE gifts (gifts are worth about $10). After receiving them, if I don't wish to receive any more books, I can return the shipping statement marked "cancel." If I don't cancel, I will receive 4 brand-new novels every month and be billed just $4.74 per book in the U.S. or $5.24 per book in Canada. That's a savings of at least 14% off the cover price! It's quite a bargain! Shipping and handling is just 50¢ per book in the U.S. and 75¢ per book in Canada.* I understand that accepting the 2 free books and gifts places me under no obligation to buy anything. I can always return a shipment and cancel at any time. Even if I never buy another book, the two free books and gifts are mine to keep forever.

154/354 HDN F4YN

Name _____ (PLEASE PRINT)

Address _____ Apt. #

City _____ State/Prov. _____ Zip/Postal Code

Signature (if under 18, a parent or guardian must sign)

Mail to the Harlequin® Reader Service:
IN U.S.A.: P.O. Box 1867, Buffalo, NY 14240-1867
IN CANADA: P.O. Box 609, Fort Erie, Ontario L2A 5X3

Want to try two free books from another line?
Call 1-800-873-8635 or visit www.ReaderService.com.

* Terms and prices subject to change without notice. Prices do not include applicable taxes. Sales tax applicable in N.Y. Canadian residents will be charged applicable taxes. Offer not valid in Quebec. This offer is limited to one order per household. Not valid for current subscribers to Harlequin American Romance books. All orders subject to credit approval. Credit or debit balances in a customer's account(s) may be offset by any other outstanding balance owed by or to the customer. Please allow 4 to 6 weeks for delivery. Offer available while quantities last.

Your Privacy—The Harlequin® Reader Service is committed to protecting your privacy. Our Privacy Policy is available online at www.ReaderService.com or upon request from the Harlequin Reader Service.

We make a portion of our mailing list available to reputable third parties that offer products we believe may interest you. If you prefer that we not exchange your name with third parties, or if you wish to clarify or modify your communication preferences, please visit us at www.ReaderService.com/consumerschoice or write to us at Harlequin Reader Service Preference Service, P.O. Box 9062, Buffalo, NY 14269. Include your complete name and address.

HARI3R

*Looking for more exciting all-American romances
like the one you just read?*

*Read on for an excerpt from
A COWBOY OF HER OWN, part of
THE CASH BROTHERS miniseries,
by Marin Thomas…*

Porter grew quiet for a minute then said, "One day I'm going to buy a ranch."

"Where?"

"I've got my eye on a place in the Fortuna Foothills."

"That's a nice area." Buying property in the foothills would require a large chunk of money, and she doubted a bank would loan it to him.

What if Porter was rustling bulls under Buddy's nose and selling them on the black market in order to finance his dream? As soon as the thought entered her mind, she pushed it away.

"So what do you say?" he said.

"What do I say about what?"

"Having a little fun before we pack it in for the night?"

"It's late. I'm not—"

"Ten o'clock isn't late." When she didn't comment, he said, "C'mon. Let your hair down."

"Are you insinuating that I'm no fun?" she teased, knowing that it was the truth.

"I'm not insinuating. I'm flat out saying it's so."

She'd show him she knew how to party. "Go ahead and stop somewhere."

Two miles later Porter pulled into the parking lot of a bar. When they entered the establishment, a wailing soprano voice threatened to wash them back outside. Karaoke night was in full swing.

"How about a game of darts?" Porter asked.

"I've never played before."

"I'll show you how to hit the bull's-eye." He laid a five-dollar bill on the bar and the bartender handed them two sets of darts. Then Porter stood behind Wendy, grasped her wrist and raised her arm.

"What are you doing?" she whispered, when his breath feathered across the back of her neck.

"Showing you how to throw." He pulled her arm back and then thrust it forward. She released the dart and it sailed across the room, hitting the wall next to the board.

"You're not a very good teacher," she said.

"I'm better at other things." The heat in his eyes stole her breath.

If you kiss him, you'll compromise your investigation.

Right now, she didn't care about her job. All she wanted was to feel Porter's mouth on hers.

He stepped back suddenly. "It's late. We'd better go."

Wendy followed, relieved one of them had come to their senses before it had been too late—she just wished it had been her and not Porter.

Look for A COWBOY OF HER OWN
by Marin Thomas, available January 2015
wherever Harlequin® American Romance®
books and ebooks are sold.

www.Harlequin.com

Homecoming Cowboy

Living on her grandfather's ranch, surrounded by her loving brothers and their families, is helping Avery Bannock put her painful past behind her.

After a decade undercover, Zane's ready to settle in Montana horse country. Now he's got to convince the gun-shy archaeologist that he's the only cowboy for her. As they work together to find out who's stealing tribal artifacts from a nearby reservation, Zane will do everything in his power to win Avery's trust…and turn their budding romance into a mission possible!

Look for
THE NEW COWBOY
by REBECCA WINTERS,

available January 2015 wherever
Harlequin® American Romance®
books and ebooks are sold.

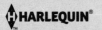

American Romance®

For their son

Texas veterinarian Delaney Blair will do *anything* to find a bone marrow donor for her four-year-old son, Nickolas. The only likely match is his Argentinean father, Dario. But Dario doesn't even know he has a son!

Delaney travels to Argentina to find him, and Dario, shocked, returns to Texas. It's not long before Nick and Dario become close. Dario can't hide the feelings he has for Delaney. Dario's family doesn't want him to be with her. But now they have to see if the love between them is strong enough to keep them together.

Look for
TEXAS MOM
by ROZ DENNY FOX,

available January 2015 wherever
Harlequin® American Romance®
books and ebooks are sold.

What she needs

Emily Miles already has plenty on her plate. She has to care for the dogs she rescues, find staff and volunteers for her shelter, not to mention raise money to keep The Wagging Tail going. She can't jeopardize the shelter by getting involved with Seth Pettit.

Seth has his own plateful: a teenage ward who hates him, an estranged family he's trying to mend fences with and a living to make in small-town Montana. Tough but delicate Emily needs a full-time partner, and that just can't be him. Not as a vet *or* a man. So why does he want to be both?

Look for
MONTANA VET
by ANN ROTH

available January 2015 wherever
Harlequin® American Romance®
books and ebooks are sold.